Gunfight at the O.K. Corral

GUNFIGHT AT THE O.K. CORRAL

Luke and Jenny Visit Tombstone

Gayle Martin

FIVE STAR LEGENDS

Five Star Publications, Inc.
P.O. Box 6698
Chandler, AZ 85246 U.S.A.
480-940-8182
Toll-Free 1-866-471-0777
www.fivestarpublications.com

Library of Congress Cataloging-in-Publication Data

Martin, Gayle 1956 –
Gunfight at the O.K. Corral: Luke and Jenny Visit Tombstone: a historical adventure / by Gayle Martin
    p.cm.
    Summary: Eight-year-old Luke and his older sister, Jenny, forget their disappointment over not going to Disneyland and about missing their father; a soldier stationed in Iraq, when a ghost takes them to Tombstone, Arizona, in 1880 for a firsthand look at its wild history.
    Includes bibliographical references.
    [1. Frontier and pioneer life – Arizona – Fiction. 2. Time travel – Fiction. 3. Ghosts – Fiction. 4. Tombstone (Ariz.) – History – Fiction. 5. Arizona – History – 1846-1911 – Fiction.] I. Title.
    PZ7.M362Gun 2007
    [Fic]—dc22
ISBN 978-1-58985-050-7
2007927279

Printed in the United States of America

EDITOR: Sherry Sterling
TYPESETTING: Arizona Living History Press, LLC
COVER ILLUSTRATION: Wes Lowe
COVER DESIGN: Arizona Living History Press, LLC

To all of my good friends in Tombstone;
Pat and Ann Marie, Dusty and Lynda, Dean, Teresa, Dru,
Carl, Liz, Kathy, and Ron, aka 'Morgan Earp'
(and anyone else whose name I may have overlooked.)
Thank you for your inspiration and encouragement.
Without your friendship and support this book
would not have been possible.

TABLE OF CONTENTS

Chapter One

Luke and Jenny Meet Virgil Earp

Luke put down his Game Boy and stared out the car window at the endless desert. This vacation was already getting boring, and they had only left home that morning.

His family had been planning a trip to Disneyland ever since Christmas, and both Luke and his older sister, Jenny, had really been looking forward to it. He spent weeks trying to decide which ride he would go on first. But then his dad was called to serve in Iraq with the Army Reserve and now nothing seemed right. His dad wouldn't be able to play video games with him, and he'd miss their backyard baseball games too. On top of that, now there would be no trip to Disneyland. His father promised they would go as soon as he returned, but that wouldn't be for at least a year. And as far as eight-year-old Luke was concerned, a year seemed like forever.

He glanced at Jenny who was looking out the window. Luke noticed that the desert was just as boring on her side as his. They were driving to Dallas to visit Grandma and Grandpa. With their father away, their mother had decided on this summer vacation. Of course, Luke and Jenny loved seeing their grandparents, but it just wasn't the same as going to Disneyland.

Their mother had also decided that they would take a few

side trips along the way. She told them they would make the trip more fun and like a real vacation. Ellen Bartlett knew that her children had been very disappointed by the recent turn of events. Of course, she missed her husband too. But she planned to make their vacation as much fun as she could.

"We're going to stop for lunch in Tombstone," she told them.

Luke watched her short blond curls move as she bobbed her head while she spoke.

"It's going to be a lot of fun and you two are really going to like it. It's an Old West town where they had that gunfight at the O.K. Corral. Remember not too long ago we saw a program about it on the History Channel."

Luke and Jenny turned to look at each other. Jenny looked just as bored with the idea of stopping in Tombstone as Luke did. He picked up his Game Boy and started to play with it again, but even that wasn't fun anymore, so he put it in one of the two backpacks that rested on the seat between them.

They arrived in Tombstone a few minutes later. It was a dusty little town with old, strange-looking buildings. Their mother found a place to park along one of the narrow streets. Luke and Jenny got out of the car, put on their backpacks, and eagerly stretched their legs. As they started walking they noticed the sidewalks were made from wooden planks. Their mother called them boardwalks. They walked around a corner.

"This is Allen Street, where all the saloons were," explained their mother. "Doesn't this remind you of the Westerns we watch on TV at home? Why, I can just imagine all those lawmen and bad guys having a shoot-out on the very street we're walking on."

Luke was certain that it would be much more fun to watch an old Western at home. In the Westerns he had seen no cars were parked along the streets. And he could plainly see that the old buildings were no longer saloons. Looking through the windows as he passed by he saw that they were just a bunch of shops selling modern-day stuff: blue jeans, t-shirts, straw cowboy hats, and coffee mugs. Luke felt his sister poke him in the ribs with her elbow.

"Look at the man over there," she whispered in his ear. "Doesn't he look like a dork?"

Luke followed Jenny's gaze across the street and saw a man dressed in western clothes. But Luke didn't think the man looked dorky at all. He looked like Kevin Costner did in that Western about range wars that he and his dad had recently watched. With that thought, he missed his dad more than ever and wished that he could have come to Tombstone with them.

"Do you have your digital camera in your backpack?" he asked. Jenny nodded. "Can I take some pictures with it? We could email them to Dad," he said.

"Your father would really like that," said their mother.

Luke took Jenny's camera and looked around. He noticed a couple of other men dressed up like cowboys, so he took a picture of them as well.

"Dad will probably think this is really cool," he said as he handed the camera back to his sister.

"Now," said their mother, "I don't know about the two of you, but I'm ready for lunch. How about you?"

"Yeah!" Both Luke and Jenny said at the same time.

Luke suddenly realized he wasn't so bored anymore. Instead, he was very hungry.

"Let's go over there!" said Jenny.

She pointed to a building across the street with big stained glass windows. The sign on the front said Big Nose Kate's Saloon.

"I think the windows are pretty," she added.

"Okay," said their mother, "but let's not stay too long."

They crossed the street, entered Big Nose Kate's Saloon, and sat down at a table near one of the stained glass windows. The place was crowded with people sitting at tables and at a wooden bar that looked like something out of a Western. A waitress wearing a blue saloon girl dress soon came to their table and took their orders. After she left Luke looked around to take it all in.

He saw several more large stained glass windows. One had a design of a man with a mustache wearing a suit, and another was of a lady wearing a high collar blouse and a big fancy hat. In front of the windows was a small stage where a man sat playing a guitar and singing old cowboy songs. And all around the walls were covered with dozens of photos of people dressed up as modern-day cowboys.

"Howdy there partner. Where are you from?"

Luke looked up and saw that a tall, middle-aged man, dressed in western clothes, had walked up to their table. He had reddish-brown hair and a dark brown mustache. And even though his large size was overpowering, his big brown eyes looked friendly.

"We're from Phoenix," said his mother. "We've just stopped to do some sightseeing on our way to Dallas to spend time with my folks."

"I see," said the man. "I thought I heard a bit of a Texas accent when you spoke. You're not by chance related to anyone in the Cowboy Gang, now are you?"

Ellen Bartlett laughed.

"No sir. They are most definitely not any kinfolk of mine."

"Well ma'am, that is certainly a relief to me. My name is Virgil Earp," he said as he extended his hand. "I'm a deputy U.S. marshal, and I live right here in Tombstone. Maybe you've heard of my brother, Wyatt Earp. He's pretty famous around here."

Luke looked at the man in amazement while nodding his head. Virgil kept talking to them.

"It sounds like you folks are just passing through. But be careful! There are plenty of outlaws around here."

Luke looked at Jenny. He knew that Wyatt Earp had

lived in Tombstone in the 1880s, so he wondered how a man from the Old West could be standing next to him. None of his friends would believe him unless he brought back some proof. He turned his gaze back at Virgil Earp.

"Mr. Virgil, would you mind letting us take a picture with you?"

"Why son, I'd be honored to have my portrait taken with you. You don't by chance work for Mr. Fly, do you?"

"Mr. Fly?" asked Luke. "Who's that?"

"Why Mr. Camillus Sidney Fly and his wife, Mollie, have a photo studio right here in Tombstone. They've taken photos all over the West, including portraits of just about everyone around here. They also own a boarding house. That's where Wyatt's buddy Doc Holliday lives."

"No sir, we don't work for Mr. Fly," said Luke. "I just wanted to take a picture of all of us with my sister's digital camera."

"A *digital camera*?" asked Virgil Earp. He paused for a moment. "Did you say a digital camera?"

Luke and Jenny nodded.

"Sounds like another one of those strange contraptions that you folks from out of town keep bringing in here. But if that's what you want to use for our portraits, then so be it," he said, with a wink and a smile.

"Would it be okay, Mom?" asked Luke.

"Sure," said his mother.

"Then why don't you folks step over here with me? There'll be more room for us."

Luke, Jenny, and their mother got up from their table and followed him across the room toward an antique piano. Along the way he explained that Big Nose Kate's Saloon had been the Grand Hotel back in the 1880s and that it had once been two stories high. But then a big fire burned down the top floor. He also told them the wood floor they were standing on was the same wood floor from the 1880s. Luke looked down at his feet, realizing he had never seen anything that old before. Maybe this stop in Tombstone wasn't going to be so bad after all.

When they got to the piano Jenny handed her camera to a passing waitress and asked if she would take their picture. As they posed with Virgil Earp Luke smiled a big smile. He was finally starting to have some fun. The waitress gave the camera back to Jenny while Luke looked around some more. His face lit up as he saw something else.

"What is that? Is that a real coffin?"

He pointed to an open coffin leaning against the wall.

"Why yes, it is," said Virgil. "That's where we do our hanging around here! And we can even take another portrait of you being hung. Would you like that?"

"Would I!" exclaimed Luke. He shot an eager glance to his mother. "Can I get hung, Mom?"

Ellen smiled. "Sure you can." She was happy that Luke had finally stopped pouting.

Once Luke was inside the coffin Virgil put a noose around Luke's neck.

"Don't worry ma'am, it's perfectly safe," he said to Ellen while Jenny took the picture. When they were finished Luke asked Jenny to show it to him.

"Awesome! Tonight I'm going to email that to Dad in Iraq."

Luke's smile suddenly faded. Just mentioning his dad made him feel sad again.

Virgil Earp noticed Luke's change in mood. He looked down at him.

"Your dad is in Iraq, son? Well, that's something we have in common."

He crouched down so his eyes would be on the same level as Luke's as put his hands on Luke's shoulders and whispered.

"Hey partner, I'm going to let you in on a little secret, but it's just between us, okay?"

Luke nodded.

"You know, when I was about your age, my dad got sent

to Viet Nam."

"He did?" asked Luke, suddenly confused.

He knew from family stories that his great uncle had been killed in Viet Nam in 1967. So he wondered how a man from the 1880s could possibly have had a father who served in Viet Nam.

"Yes, sir," replied Virgil. "It was toward the end of the war, and he wasn't gone that long. But back then I felt just like you. I thought my dad was going to be gone forever. And would you like to know something else?"

"What?" asked Luke.

"A lot of folks around here have family members in the service. And some of them are serving in Iraq and Afghanistan too," said Virgil.

"Really?" asked Luke.

"You bet partner. We have to remember that our troops have a very important job to do. They're serving our country. And we have to stay strong so they can do their jobs and not worry about us. Do you understand what I'm saying, partner?"

Luke nodded. Virgil looked over at Ellen and Jenny, then he turned back to Luke.

"Now the way I see it is until your dad returns, you're the man in the family, so you need to set a good example. Can you do that for me?"

Luke looked into Virgil's eyes, smiled, and nodded his head. Virgil stood up and extended his hand.

"That's my buddy! Give me five!"

Luke laughed and slapped his hand down on Virgil's.

"There you go, partner. Now let's escort your womenfolk back to your table."

On the way, they passed a metal spiral staircase that went downstairs. Luke stopped in front of it.

"What's that?" he asked Virgil.

"Why, that's the staircase that goes down to where the Swamper used to live," said Virgil.

"The Swamper! That sounds like some sort of monster!" Virgil laughed.

"Don't worry, son, he's not a monster."

He explained that the Swamper was a handyman who took care of the Grand Hotel in the 1880s. He was a good worker who kept to himself and lived in a room in the basement. Later on, folks discovered that he had dug a secret tunnel from his room into one of the silver mines.

"It's believed by some that his secret silver treasure is still buried somewhere down there, and that his ghost haunts this building to this very day."

Luke's eyes suddenly opened wide. A ghost!

Virgil laughed again.

"Don't worry son, he's a very friendly ghost. He just wants to watch over this place."

They returned to their table and the instant Luke took his seat the waitress brought his burger and fries.

"You folks enjoy your stay in Tombstone."

And with that Virgil Earp tipped his hat and went to talk to the people at another table.

"That wasn't the real Virgil Earp, you know," said Jenny as she flipped her long, blond ponytail over her shoulder and picked up her chicken sandwich.

"The real Virgil Earp died a long time ago. He was just an actor or somebody they have here to pretend to be Virgil Earp."

Jenny was going be starting the fifth grade that fall and she thought of herself as very grown up. But Luke wasn't listening to her. As he ate his lunch he couldn't help thinking about the ghost of the Swamper.

Chapter Two
The Ghosts of Tombstone

After lunch Luke, Jenny, and their mother strolled the streets of Tombstone. Soon they came upon an old, pink building with arched doorways. It was called the Bird Cage Theater. Luke noticed a sign posted on the sidewalk in front of the theater. It read: "Curly Bill Brocius shot Marshal Fred White here on October 28, 1880."

"What's up with that?" he asked.

When no one answered he turned around and realized that his mother and sister had already gone inside. He quickly followed and stepped into what must have been the theater lobby. It was a narrow room with an ornately carved wooden bar in front of a large mirror at one end. The room was filled with t-shirts and books for sale. At the other end stood several old clocks and a large painting of a woman wearing what looked like a pair of pajamas. He looked back toward the bar and noticed a blond man with kind blue eyes standing behind it.

"Welcome to the Bird Cage Theater, folks. Would you like to see the museum?"

"How much is it?" asked his mother.

While she talked to the man Luke noticed a strange smell.

9

He wrinkled his nose. Then he saw that Jenny had noticed it too.

"This building must be really old," she said. "It smells musty. Sometimes old buildings get a musty smell to them."

Luke decided he didn't like the smell of old buildings. He walked up to the bar and stood next to his mother, then smelled something else. Cigar smoke.

"Was someone just smoking a cigar in here?" he asked.

The man shook his head and smiled.

"No, sir," he said, "It's just them."

"Who are they?" asked Luke.

"Why the ghosts. Did you know that the Bird Cage Theater is one of the most haunted buildings in America?" asked the man.

Luke and Jenny shook their heads.

"Back in the 1880s, this building was a saloon and gambling hall as well as a theater, and at that time the men smoked cigars. But a lot of murders happened in this place. That's why it's so haunted. Sometimes, when the ghosts are around, you can smell cigar smoke or lilac perfume. That's the kind of perfume the ladies who worked here wore. Lots of strange things happen here at the Birdcage. Some folks say that when you walk past here at night, after everything has closed, you can hear piano music and laughter coming out of this building."

Luke's eyes widened. More ghosts.

The man went on to tell them that in the 1880s the wall that separated the bar from the stage was not there, and that the woman in the painting had been one of the many performers at the Bird Cage Theater. She went by the names Fatima and Little Egypt, and she had been a famous belly dancer. He explained that belly dancing had been a popular form of entertainment back then and that Fatima had thought so much of the people of Tombstone that she had the painting made just for them and had given it to the town as a gift. Then he pointed out some bullet holes in the painting, as well as one in the bar, and told them that a lot of guns had been fired inside the Bird Cage back in its Wild West days.

"Let's go inside and have a look at the museum," said their mother.

The man came around from the bar and opened a door. This led into a big, dimly lit room where they saw the old stage with an old piano in front of it. This had been the rest of the original theater. Now it was a museum filled with antiques.

Jenny grabbed Luke by the arm.

"Look Luke! Up there!"

She pointed to one of the theater boxes above them.

"A ghost is sitting right there, and he's watching you!"

She started to laugh.

Luke looked up to see the old theater's box seats and indeed, a man was sitting in one of the boxes looking at him. His jaw dropped. He noticed that the wooden ceiling was dotted with bullet holes. He knew then that the Wild West really had been wild, just like in the movies. Only this was all too real. No wonder the place was so creepy.

"Jenny you stop that this instant!" her mother scolded. "That's no ghost. That's just a dummy—part of the display. They put it there to show you what the people coming to the theater would have worn back then. There's no such thing as ghosts. The people around here just like to tell stories. Now let's look around the museum. We can see some of the things that people really used back then."

Luke sighed in relief. As they looked around the museum, Jenny took her camera out again.

"Let's have some fun, Luke," she whispered, not wanting their mother to hear. "I'm going to take a picture of the dummy in the box, and we can email it to Dad tonight and tell him it's a real ghost. Don't you think he'd get a kick out of it?"

Luke snickered under his breath as he looked back at

her and nodded. If their father couldn't be there with them, maybe they could play a little joke on him. As long as they meant no harm and admitted it in the end, it would be okay. Everyone in the family had a good sense of humor.

After Jenny took her picture they walked around the building for a while longer, taking in relics from the past: from beautifully carved wooden desks to rusted metal kitchen utensils, and old photos of people who had once performed in the Birdcage and of people who had lived in Tombstone long ago. Backstage they saw a horse-drawn hearse. Then they went down a narrow flight of steps leading into a small poker room. There they found a poker table covered with poker chips and playing cards.

"It looks like everyone just got up and left in the middle of a card game," said their mother.

The longer they spent looking around the old theater, the more Luke got an uneasy feeling. From the moment he came in he felt as if he was being watched, and a couple of times he thought he saw someone moving past him. But every time he looked around he saw that no one else was in the room except for him, his mother, and his sister. He noticed too that in a few places the air felt very cold. He even felt a couple of cold breezes blow across his face and arms but he decided not to mention it. He did not want to take the chance of upsetting his mother again. When they finally left the building Luke breathed a sigh of relief.

Back on the boardwalk Jenny stopped to look at the picture she had taken.

"That's strange," she said. "Luke, look at this."

Luke looked at the image on the back of Jenny's camera and saw the top of the theater box, but the display of the man sitting in it was covered by some strange fog. It was something they had not seen when Jenny took the picture.

"Luke, do you think that building really is haunted?" she asked.

"That's enough, Jenny!" scolded their mother.

Not only was she becoming very annoyed, she was beginning to worry that with all the ghost stories the children were hearing they might not be able to sleep that night.

"Let me have a look at that, please."

She took Jenny's camera and looked at the photo. She shook the puzzled look off her face and shrugged her shoulders.

"That probably happened because it was so dark that your camera didn't work right, Jenny. Either that box was up too high for you to get a good shot, or the flash reflected some dust in the air, but it most certainly is not a ghost."

She handed the camera back to Jenny and decided to get the children's minds off of ghosts, once and for all.

"So, who wants ice cream?" she asked.

"We do!" replied Luke and Jenny together.

They soon found a little shop where their mother bought ice cream cones for them and a fancy iced coffee drink for herself. Jenny got strawberry ice cream while Luke got chocolate. They sat down on one of many the benches on the boardwalk to finish their treats.

"You two stay right here and eat the rest of your ice cream," said their mother as she finished her iced coffee. "I want to look around the stores for a few minutes and find something for your dad and for Grandma and Grandpa. I won't be but a few minutes, and then we'll go. Will you two be okay?"

"Sure Mom, we'll be fine," said Jenny. "You said I'm almost old enough to baby-sit, remember?"

"Indeed, I did. So you look after your brother, and I'll be back in a flash."

As they watched their mother walk down the boardwalk Luke pulled his Game Boy out from his backpack. He noticed a sudden chill in the air.

"Brrrr!" he said, shivering.

He looked over at Jenny. She had goosebumps on her arms.

"Are you cold, too, Jenny?" he asked.

"Uh huh," she replied. "That ice cream must have been really cold."

"Yeah," said Luke, "but it was really good."

He turned on the Game Boy and had just started playing when it died.

"It's busted!" he exclaimed.

"Here, let me see it," said Jenny.

She grabbed it away from him.

"That's weird. You recharged the battery, didn't you?"

"Duh," replied Luke.

She fiddled around some more.

"You're right. It's completely dead. You must have forgotten to shut it off, and now you've run down the battery."

"No way!" exclaimed Luke.

"Well then you managed to break it. And Mom is going to get pretty mad at you!"

Before Luke could reply they heard a strange voice behind them.

"What seems to be the trouble?"

Luke and Jenny looked up to see a rugged looking man with a graying mustache looking down at them. He was wearing the strangest looking old clothes that either Luke or Jenny had ever seen. His well-worn pants were dark brown and baggy. They looked like they were made out of wool and they were held up by worn leather suspenders. He wore a red shirt and on his head was a beat up, brown felt hat with a flat rim.

"My Game Boy won't work," said Luke.

"Your what?" asked the man.

"My Game..." but before he could finish his sentence Jenny interrupted.

"Everything's fine. Thank you for asking. But we're not supposed to talk to strangers."

"I'm not a stranger," said man. "I was standing right next to you in Big Nose Kate's. I heard that guy who pretends to be Virgil Earp tell you about me. When you heard my name, you said it sounded like a monster."

"I didn't see you in there," said Luke. "Besides, how do you know that man wasn't Virgil Earp? And how would you know what he said to me? Like my sister just told you, you're a stranger and we don't talk to strangers."

The man laughed.

"That man who works in there is pretty good, and we all like him because he keeps our memories alive for folks like you who come and visit Tombstone. But he's no Virgil Earp. I knew the real Virgil Earp. You see, I'm the Swamper."

Jenny spoke up.

"I get it. You're another actor, only you're pretending to be the Swamper."

But something about that man just wasn't quite right and she was getting nervous. She stood up and handed the Game Boy back to Luke.

"Put this back in your backpack," she whispered to him.

While Luke did as he was told she looked around for a policeman, their mother, or anyone else who could help them. While she was looking she noticed that none of the other tourists walking by seemed to notice this strange man who was talking to them.

"No, young lady. I'm not an actor," said the man. "I really am the Swamper. And I really did live downstairs at the Grand Hotel. Oh what a grand and beautiful place it was! Today it's called Big Nose Kate's."

Luke and Jenny looked closer at the man. Then they both saw something else that was very strange about him. He had a faint white, misty glow around him, and they could see through him. They looked at each other as shivers ran up their spines.

"Luke," whispered Jenny, "are you thinking what I'm thinking?"

"Yep," whispered her brother back, "I think the man is a ghost."

The Swamper knew the children were getting frightened, so he decided to ease their fears.

"Actually, I prefer to think of myself as a spirit person. It has a nicer ring to it, don't you think? The word 'ghost' sounds too much like Halloween."

Luke and Jenny were still too surprised to speak.

"Oh don't worry. I'm a very friendly spirit person. In fact, I'm not that different from when I was flesh and blood. It's just that nowadays most people can't see me. Sometimes that makes me feel pretty lonely. So while I was watching you in Big Nose Kate's, I got the feeling that you two were sad about something, and I thought maybe I could help."

Finally Luke spoke up.

"We were supposed to go to Disneyland this year for our vacation. Then our dad got sent to Iraq. He's in the Army, and we really miss him."

"You don't say," said the Swamper.

He scratched his chin as if he were deep in thought.

"I know about serving in the Army. In my day, we lived through the Civil War. And when I was young it seemed liked everyone's father, or uncle, or older brother went off to fight. It was a sad, sad time."

"Well, Disneyland is like this magic place," said Luke, wanting to change the subject, "and they have all kinds of adventure rides there. I don't want to hurt your feelings, but it's a lot more exciting than this place."

"I bet you're right," said the Swamper. "Tombstone is pretty dull these days. But in my time it was different. Why back then, Tombstone was the biggest city between St. Louis and San Francisco. You know, at one point nearly 10,000 people lived here. And it was wild—oh it was wild. You saw all those bullet holes in the ceiling at the Bird Cage Theater, didn't you?"

Luke and Jenny nodded.

"Well, that should give you a clue as to how wild this place once was." He paused. "Hey! I've got an idea! You say

16

you want an adventure? I could take you on an adventure you'll never forget. How would you like to travel back to my time and see what Tombstone was really like?"

Jenny spoke up.

"That sounds really nice, but our mom is going to be back any second now, and then we'll leave."

"Oh, don't worry about that," said the Swamper. "I'll have you right back here in this very spot so fast nobody will even notice that you were gone."

Luke and Jenny saw a bright flash that looked like lightning. All the buildings suddenly looked very, very different.

Chapter Three

The Streets of Old Tombstone

Jenny looked back at her brother, who was still seated on the bench. Looking into the window behind Luke she saw that everything had changed. What had been a store was now a saloon, filled with men dressed in western clothes playing pool.

"That's Campbell & Hatch's," said the Swamper. "It's a very popular place. In fact, I'll be taking you in there later to show you something."

Luke wasn't listening. He was marveling at the horses that had replaced the parked cars. He jumped off the bench to have a better look.

"Cool!" he said as he stepped into the street.

"Luke! Look out!" shouted Jenny.

A man on a horse was quickly coming up behind Luke. She raced into the street and grabbed her brother by the arm to pull him to safety, but it was too late. The man and horse were already bearing down on Luke. Then, to her surprise, they rode right through him—as if Luke wasn't there.

"What the..."

Jenny was so surprised that she could not finish her sentence. The Swamper started to laugh.

"What was that?" asked Luke.

"That man on the horse rode right though you! Didn't you see it? Didn't you feel anything?" exclaimed Jenny.

Luke looked puzzled.

"No, I didn't," he said. "I heard you shouting at me, and I felt you grab my arm. When I looked back, I saw a man on a horse in front of me. Where the heck did they come from?"

The Swamper spoke up.

"No one can see you because you're not really here. You're seeing things from the past as they really happened, but no one in the past can see you. That way, you can't do anything that would change history."

The three began walking the streets of old Tombstone. The streets were full of people: some walking down boardwalks, others on horseback or driving horse-drawn wagons. The men were either dressed in old-fashioned working clothes like the Swamper, or wore fine suits similar to the business suits their father wore to work, only these men also wore top hats or derby hats. Almost all the men had mustaches. The ladies wore long dresses with long sleeves and high collars and all kinds of fancy feathered hats. Tombstone in the 1880s was certainly a busy place. Jenny was glad that none of the townspeople could see her or Luke. She suddenly felt out of place walking around wearing a modern-day shirt and shorts.

"I get it," she said. "I've seen TV shows about this sort of thing. You know, people traveling to different times and meeting people who live there"

"TV," echoed the Swamper. "I sometimes watch the TV sets in Big Nose Kate's. We sure didn't have anything like that in my time. But you're about to learn that real-life adventures can be much more exciting than watching TV. The man that just rode through Luke was Ike Clanton. He's part of the Cowboy Gang."

"The Cowboy Gang?" asked Jenny.

"Yes indeed," said the Swamper. "The Cowboys are a bunch of outlaws who cause all kinds of problems around here. Mostly they steal cattle and horses. And they can be a pretty tough bunch to deal with if you should happen to get in their way. Some folks around here see them as bad guys, but other folks see them as heroes. In fact, the people of our town are pretty divided over them."

"But isn't stealing wrong?" asked Jenny.

"Of course it is," said the Swamper. "It's just that some folks around here don't see it as stealing. You see, most of the Cowboys came from former Confederate states, including Texas. This is my personal take on it. Do either one of you remember the story of the Alamo?"

"Sure," said Jenny. "We learned about it last year in my social studies class. The Alamo is in Texas. Men who wanted Texas to become a free country ended up in the Alamo, surrounded by the Mexican Army and General Santa Ana, but they all got killed in the end."

"That's right," said the Swamper. "Only the Cowboy Gang members didn't learn about it in their social studies class. It happened during their parents' and grandparents' day and it's still a very personal and bitter memory to them. Because of what happened at the Alamo, a lot of folks might agree with me that they probably don't think they're doing anything wrong by stealing cattle from Mexico. So that's why some folks around here think they're heroes."

"I see," said Jenny. "But I still don't think it's right."

"Plenty of other folks around here would agree with you, Jenny," said the Swamper. "You see, Tombstone is a mining town, or a boom town, and people have come here from all around to seek their fortune in the silver mines. Some are good people and some are bad people."

"I noticed there are a lot more people here now, in the past, than in our time," said Jenny, "How big is this place now?"

"Let's see," said the Swamper, "I've just brought you back to the year 1880, and right now I believe there are about 4,000 or so people living here. And everyday the stagecoach brings new arrivals. That may seem like a very small town to the two of you, but Tombstone is considered a big city in our day. And just think, Arizona is still a territory. It won't become a state until 1912."

"How did it all start?" asked Luke.

"I thought you'd never ask," said the Swamper. "It all started a few years ago, that is, by the time we're standing in right now. See that man over there, the one with the curly hair down to his shoulders and the black mustache and beard?

Luke and Jenny nodded as the Swamper pointed to a man standing across the street.

"His name is Ed Schieffelin. A few years ago he was out prospecting in the hills just outside of town. But this is Apache country—a very dangerous place to be—so someone said, 'Ed, if you go there, all you'll find is your tombstone.' But do you know what he found?"

Luke and Jenny shook their heads.

"Why, he found the mother lode of all silver! That means he found a very rich vain of ore. Now Ed has a good sense of humor, so he called his first two claims The Tombstone and The Graveyard. Then he left for a while to bring back his brother, Albert, and another man called Richard Gird. The next thing they knew, prospectors were crawling all over the place, and then a city sprang up, and then in 1879 the city became the town of Tombstone. And that's how a boom town is born."

"I see," said Luke. " And where did all these other people come from?"

"Well, businessmen have come to open up stores and restaurants and theaters and saloons. But you know, it's almost like the Civil War all over again because most of the townspeople came from Union states, but most of the Cowboy Gang came from Confederate states like Texas. The Cowboys and the miners are good customers for the saloon keepers and shop owners, and they're known to be pretty good Indian fighters too. We're still in Apache country, so if we were to ever have trouble with the Indians, the Cowboys could be a big help. So that's why the townsfolk who don't agree with them put up with them."

He tapped Jenny on the shoulder.

"Look over there. See those two man wearing the badges standing in front of the Crystal Palace Saloon?"

Jenny nodded.

"The one on the left is Virgil Earp. He's the deputy U.S. marshal. The man standing next to him is our town marshal, Fred White."

"Funny, he doesn't look like that guy we saw at Big Nose Kate's," said Luke.

"Actors," said the Swamper, shaking his head. "Five Earp Brothers live in Tombstone right now, including the famous Wyatt. Morgan Earp is Virgil's deputy; Wyatt is working for Wells Fargo; the oldest brother, James, is working as a bartender; and Warren, the youngest brother, will be coming along to help Wyatt. The Earps have come here as businessmen, hoping to find their fortunes like so many others. And they've brought along a friend. His name is Doc Holliday, and he's about one of the meanest men you could ever meet. Doc has brought along his girlfriend, Big Nose Kate."

"So there really was a Big Nose Kate," said Jenny. "Why did they call her that? Did she have a big nose?"

The Swamper laughed.

"Not really. She goes by the name Kate Elder around here. Her family was from Hungary, and some folks say she comes from Hungarian royalty."

"Wow!" said Jenny. "You mean she's a real-life princess?"

The Swamper laughed.

"Now I don't know about that for certain, but I do know she has a very bad habit. She likes to stick her nose into other people's business. That's why they call her Big Nose Kate."

"I've heard of Doc Holliday," said Luke, "But why is he such a mean man?"

"Well, that's a sad story, Luke," said the Swamper. "John Henry Holliday came from a good family in Georgia and he became a dentist—a very good dentist, too. Then he got very, very sick—too sick to be a dentist anymore. Doc came down with something called consumption. It gets in your lungs, makes you very sick, and there's no cure. If you catch it you'll die from it."

"Oh no!" exclaimed Luke. "I don't want to catch it!"

"You don't have to worry, Luke," said the Swamper. "In your time, consumption is known as tuberculosis. And in your time it's very rare and your doctors can treat it. But in the 1880s consumption was a very bad thing that killed a lot of people. They could get it if a sick person coughed on them. That's why your mother tells you to cover your mouth when you cough if you're sick."

"Poor Doc Holliday. No wonder he's so mean. I feel bad for him," said Luke. "So what's he doing if he can't be a dentist anymore?"

"Doc's become a gambling man, and you don't ever want to get on his bad side," warned the Swamper. "Why, if you were to make him angry, Doc could be a very dangerous man!"

Jenny shuddered. She thought it was a good thing that Doc Holliday couldn't see her or her brother. The Swamper must have read her mind.

"Don't worry about Doc Holliday, Jenny," he said. "He may be mean, but only to bad men, like the kind of men who cheat at card games. He may not like any of the Cowboys, but he really does like children. I know he would like both you and your brother."

The Swamper pointed to two other men on another street corner.

"Now if you look over there you'll see some of the Cowboys," said the Swamper. "That man over there, the one wearing the sash around his waist, is Johnny Ringo. He and Doc Holliday really hate one another. In fact, Johnny Ringo is one of the most dangerous outlaws around."

Jenny said, "I saw a movie about Tombstone in which all

23

of the Cowboys wore red sashes. But I don't see anyone else wearing one."

The Swamper laughed.

"That was a movie, Jenny. In reality, most outlaws don't wear anything that would make them stand out from everybody else. Next to Johnny Ringo, the man with the dark curly hair wearing two gun belts with the sombrero hat, is Curly Bill Brocius. He's every bit as bad as the rest of them. In fact, something very, very bad is about to happen between Curly Bill and Marshal White."

Chapter Four

The Shooting of Marshal Fred White

The day suddenly turned into a dark night.

"What happened?" exclaimed Luke.

"Think of this as a guided tour through history," said the Swamper, "and on this journey it may be daytime one minute, and nighttime the next. On this stop I want to show you something very important that happened in our town. It's the very early morning of October 28, 1880, and..."

The Swamper was suddenly interrupted by the sound of gunshots ringing in the night air.

"What was that?" asked Luke and Jenny at the same time.

"Look over there, Jenny," said Luke, as he pointed to the gunfire flashes. They saw a group of men about a block away. The men were pointing their guns in the air and laughing and shooting.

"Someone else heard it, too, Luke," said the Swamper. "Look behind you. Here comes Wyatt Earp himself."

They turned to see Wyatt Earp running out of a nearby saloon. He ran past them as he followed the sight of the gun flashes up the street.

"Follow me," said the Swamper, running behind Wyatt Earp.

They heard more shots and saw more gunfire flashes in the night sky. They followed Wyatt as he met up with two other men who were crouched behind a building.

"Those two men are Wyatt's brother, Morgan, and their

friend, Fred Dodge," explained the Swamper.

"Morgan, I'm unarmed," said Wyatt to his brother. "Can you loan me your pistol?"

"Sorry Wyatt, I can't. I may need it."

"That's a brother for you," said Jenny.

"Here Wyatt, you can borrow mine," said Fred Dodge.

As Fred Dodge handed Wyatt his pistol they heard another voice shout in the darkness.

"I'm an officer of the law. Give me your weapon."

"Over here," said the Swamper.

He was motioning Luke and Jenny to follow Wyatt. As they came around the building, they saw that Fred White, the Tombstone town marshal, had caught up with one of the Cowboys on a vacant lot.

"That's Curly Bill," said the Swamper. "He and his friends spent a little too much time in a saloon tonight and they've had too much to drink. When they left the saloon, they thought it would be fun to shoot at the moon and stars. Now Fred White is going to try to arrest Curly Bill."

Curly Bill had drawn his gun and pointed it at Marshal White. Wyatt Earp snuck up behind Curly Bill and threw his arms around him. As he did Fred White grabbed the barrel of Curly Bill's gun.

"Now I told you to give me that pistol!"

Luke suddenly realized that the vacant lot they were standing in was where the Bird Cage Theater now stood. Then he remembered the sign he read in front of the Bird Cage—he knew what was about to happen.

"Oh no!"

He reached over to grab the barrel of Curly Bill's gun and pull it away. But when he grabbed it he saw his hand go right through, as if the gun barrel wasn't really there. Then Marshal White jerked on Curly Bill's gun, which went off, hitting him and setting his clothes on fire.

"I'm hit!" he yelled as he fell to the ground.

Wyatt Earp immediately hit Curly Bill over the head with

his borrowed pistol, knocking him to the ground. He reached down and grabbed him by the collar.

"Get up!" he curtly ordered, yanking Curly Bill to his feet.

When Curly Bill got up he appeared to be dazed and confused.

"What have I done?" he asked as he stumbled around trying to get his footing, "I haven't done anything to be arrested for."

In the meantime Morgan and Fred Dodge ran up.

"You two put out the fire on Marshal White's clothes," shouted Wyatt.

Other townspeople quickly gathered around the scene. A few of them picked up Fred White and carried him to the town doctor while Wyatt and his other brother, Virgil, took Curly Bill away. After everyone left and the street was empty, Jenny started to cry.

"That poor man," she said, "What's going to happened to him?"

"Well, it's a sad story, Jenny," said the Swamper. "Marshal White dies a couple of days later. And the people of Tombstone, in honor of their fallen marshal, passed a city law that forbids anyone other than an officer of the law to carry a loaded gun in Tombstone. And do you know what? That law is still in effect, even in your time."

"I saw what was going to happen," said Luke. "I tried to pull the gun away so it wouldn't hurt Marshal White, but I couldn't. It went right through my fingers."

"I know you tried to save Marshal White, Luke. But that would have changed history, and that you cannot do," said the Swamper.

"That Curly Bill is a horrible, horrible man!" exclaimed Jenny. "I hope they hang him for what he did."

She heard a voice behind her.

"You're right Jenny. I did a lot of very bad things in my time. But you have to believe me when I tell you that even

27

though it was all my fault, it really was a terrible accident."

She turned and saw Curly Bill standing behind her. But he looked different. He had that same strange white glow about him that the Swamper had. And, just like the Swamper, she could see right through him. She looked at the Swamper.

"I thought you said none of them could see us."

"We can't see you in life," explained Curly Bill. "But I'm speaking to you in your time. I guess that makes me a spirit person, too."

He looked at Jenny and saw that she had been crying. He reached into his vest pocket to find a handkerchief but couldn't find one. He checked his other pockets and still came up empty. He looked up.

"I can't find my handkerchief. Fred, do you have one?"

"Sure do. Right here." said another voice.

Jenny turned to see the ghost of Fred White. He smiled and gave her his handkerchief. Then he looked at the Swamper.

"Why don't Bill and I take it from here?"

"Good," said the Swamper. "I need to go check on their mother. I'll be right back." The Swamper vanished into thin air.

"That is so totally awesome!" exclaimed Luke.

Fred White said, "Come here, Luke and Jenny. Let's sit down on the boardwalk for a few minutes. Curly Bill and I want to explain something to you about what the two of you just saw."

Luke and Jenny sat down on the boardwalk between Curly Bill and Marshal White. Jenny looked up at Fred White, who sat next to her, and noticed how young he was.

"I'm so sorry that you died so young."

"That's what we wanted to talk to you about, Jenny," said Marshal White. "I let my temper get the best of me that night. The Cowboys were causing trouble and I got angry. And because I was angry I wasn't thinking right and I did something very foolish. Bill's gun was pointed right at me

28

when I reached over and jerked it. It was a stupid mistake and I paid for it with my life."

"But it was my fault too," added Curly Bill. "Luke, Jenny, I want you to believe me when I tell you that what you saw really was an accident. My friends and I had way too much to drink that night. When we came out of that saloon, my friends thought it would be fun to try to shoot the moon and stars. I didn't think so and I tried to stop them, but I couldn't. We were all too drunk, and no one was listening to anything anyone else had to say. By the time the marshal here caught me, I didn't know what I was doing. You just saw it. When my gun went off, I really didn't know what had happened. You do believe me, don't you?"

Bill looked at Luke and Jenny, and they both nodded.

"Wyatt took me to jail that night, and a few weeks later a hearing was held for me in Tucson. You know, I could have been hung if I had been found guilty! But only one bullet had been fired from my gun that night, and that was the one that accidentally hit Marshal White."

"And I signed a deathbed statement saying that the shooting was an accident," added Marshal White.

"But that still doesn't mean that I'm not responsible for what happened to Fred here." said Curly Bill.

Bill paused for a moment, as if he were in deep thought. He sighed and began to look very sad.

"There's something else I need to say to you as well."

He paused again, trying to find the right words.

"You see, we're all human, and we all do things we know are wrong. But some of us go way too far, and we do things that are very, very wrong. That's what I did. I stole from people and I even murdered people! But at the time, I was arrogant enough to think that I could get away with it. Then I found out, the hard way, that you can never get away with it! When you set out to do wrong, it always catches up to you. And because of the all the mean and rotten things I did to people while I was alive I'm not at peace now. So I've decided to do something about it.

"I can never go back and erase the wrongs I've done. But I can do whatever I can now to help the living. Like coming here and talking to the two of you about my mistakes. This helps me on my journey to make up for all those bad things I did in the past. Then, someday, I'll find peace."

"Well, I'm back," said the Swamper as he appeared in the darkness. "Their mother is still busy shopping, and I've plenty more to show them."

He looked at Curly Bill.

"I think I'll start with how you celebrated after you were set free from the killing of the marshal."

"Oh no!" exclaimed Curly Bill, "Not that!"

"Yes, that," the Swamper gleefully told Curly Bill as Luke and Jenny laughed.

"I'll bet this is going to be good," said Luke.

"Oh, it is," replied Curly Bill sheepishly.

"By the way Bill, a baseball game's about to start on the television set at Big Nose Kate's," said the Swamper.

"Who's playing?" asked Bill.

"The Texas Rangers and the Oakland A's," replied the Swamper.

Curly Bill jumped up.

"How about that Fred?"

He laughed as he slapped Marshal White's shoulder.

"Just like old times! It's Texans against Northern Californians."

He looked down at Luke and Jenny and tipped his sombrero.

"It was a pleasure meeting the two of you. Enjoy your visit with your grandparents in Dallas."

He turned back to Fred White.

"Would you like to join me in watching the game, Fred?"

"Don't mind if I do," said Marshal White.

Before he got up he looked at Luke and Jenny.

"What happened between Bill and me is over and done with. I forgave him a long time ago. Now that Curly Bill is trying to make up for all the bad things he did when he was alive, I sometimes try to help him out."

He rose and stood up on the boardwalk.

"It was nice meeting you, Luke and Jenny. We must be on our way."

"I'll bet you two didn't know that baseball was very popular in Tombstone," said the Swamper.

Luke and Jenny shook their heads.

"Why, back in the days of the Old West, Tombstone had its very own baseball team."

"Really?" asked Luke.

"You bet," said the Swamper.

"By the way, we ghosts love television," added Curly Bill. "And with all those cable sports channels we can watch all the baseball we want. And since none of you can see us we can sit right in front of the screen and yell at the umpires as loud as we want. I wish we'd had it in our time. Maybe we would have gotten ourselves into less trouble. Don't you think so, Marshal White?"

"I seriously doubt that, Bill," said Marshal White as he shook his head, "But if you don't stop your yapping, we're going to miss the opening pitch."

The two walked away, slowly fading into the darkness.

Jenny looked down and saw she was still holding Marshal White's handkerchief.

"Hey wait!" she yelled, "You forgot this!"

But it was too late. Curly Bill and Fred White were gone.

"I guess I'll have to give this back to him later," she said as she tucked it into her backpack.

"So what was it that Curly Bill didn't want us to see?" asked Luke.

"Thought you'd never ask," said the Swamper as they suddenly found themselves in a church, with the preacher in the middle of a sermon.

Chapter Five
Curly Bill Goes to Church

Luke and Jenny looked around. They were now sitting on a wooden pew at the back of a little church. It didn't look that different from the church their family went to. It was a just a bit smaller and the people were dressed in their Sunday best— the men in suits, the ladies in long dresses. The men had removed their hats. Jenny looked over at the Swamper and noticed he was taking off his hat too.

"It's considered bad manners for a gentleman to wear his hat indoors," he said, "especially in church."

He went on to tell them that this little church was in the town of Contention, a few miles away from Tombstone.

"I've never heard of a town called Contention," said Luke.

"It doesn't exist anymore, Luke," said the Swamper. "About all that is left of Contention are a few foundations. Now watch carefully. You're about to see something that's truly shocking."

Luke and Jenny turned to watch the preacher standing at the pulpit. He was busy preaching his sermon.

"And the day of the Lord will come like a thief in the night..."

He was suddenly interrupted by the sound of the church doors bursting open. Luke and Jenny turned around to see Curly Bill and one of his Cowboy friends walking into the church with their guns drawn. The congregation looked stunned. Some of them were so pale that they looked like they might faint.

"Bill's been celebrating his release from jail. He and his friend have been out drinking all night," said the Swamper. "They've already caused a lot of trouble, and now they're going to see how much more they can get into."

No one said a word as Curly Bill and his friend walked up the aisle to the preacher, who still stood behind the pulpit. They looked at one another for a moment, then Curly Bill finally spoke up.

"Reverend, I've heard it said by folks around here that you're a good man and that you're strong in your Christian faith, so I've decided to come here and see for myself. Please, go on telling these good folks about this Lord of yours and pay no attention to me."

"Whatever he's up to won't be good," whispered Jenny to her brother.

"Yeah! That's probably why he's having to make up for things as a ghost," Luke whispered back. "And look, they're not even taking off their hats."

Curly Bill kept talking to the preacher.

"Now you stand perfectly still."

The minister nodded.

"And as long as you don't move, you won't get hurt. But if you do, well then, I guess this congregation will have to do without a preacher. Now, go back to what you were preaching."

The minister took a deep breath and began to speak.

"And the Day of the Lord…"

His words were suddenly broken up by the loud, banging sound of gunfire. Curly Bill and his friend were firing their guns at the preacher. But he stood very still and kept on preaching while the Cowboys shot out some of the church windows. The walls behind him and on both sides began to collect bullet holes too. Some of the shots only missed the preacher's head by an inch or two. Luke and Jenny held their breath as they watched and Jenny covered her ears. But somehow, amid the noise of all the gunfire, the preacher managed to finish his sermon. The congregation sat and watched in horror. None of them were armed, and Curly Bill and his friend were much too dangerous for any of them to try to take on.

After the minister was finished Curly Bill looked at him.

"Well now. You have shown all of us that indeed you are a man of strong faith and that you know your Bible quite well. Now step down here my good friend."

The minister hesitated.

"It's all right," said Curly Bill. "Come on down from behind that pulpit so we can all see you."

The minister slowly stepped down as Curly Bill gave his next command.

"Now dance for us, my good friend."

The minister grew pale.

"I can't dance," he said. "It's against the teachings of my faith!"

Curly Bill smiled.

"Oh, that's all right. Somehow I think your Lord will understand."

Then his faced hardened and he raised his gun.

"But you will dance for me!"

The minister knew then that he had no choice. If he did not dance for Curly Bill, then he would certainly find himself facing his gun once again. Only this time he knew that Curly Bill would not miss. So he began to slowly shuffle his feet, then he shuffled them a little faster. He kept going until Bill finally told him it was time to stop.

Curly Bill turned to face the congregation, who had been sitting in silent fear. By this time Jenny had seen enough. She got up from the pew and stormed to the front of the church.

"What is she doing?" asked the Swamper.

He knew Curly Bill could not see her and would not be

able to hurt her. He just wondered what she was up to.

"I've had enough of you!" she shouted at Curly Bill. "Do you think that picking on people who can't defend themselves makes you a big man? Well, it doesn't! It just makes you a bully! And do you know what bullies are? Losers! You're a loser, Curly Bill Brocius! That's spelled L- O- S - E - R!"

She kicked Curly Bill in the shins. Luke snickered as he watched Jenny's foot go right through Curly Bill's boot. Next she looked over at Bill's friend who was standing nearby.

"And that goes for you, too. You're both a couple of losers!"

"Well Luke, your sister certainly has a lot of spunk," said the Swamper.

Luke looked a little embarrassed.

"Yeah. She's bossy because she's the oldest."

"But she's right about one thing, Luke," said the Swamper. "Picking on people who are weaker than you doesn't make you strong at all. It just makes you a coward."

In the meantime, Curly Bill, totally unaware of Jenny, looked at the people in the congregation.

"You people do indeed have a very fine man to lead you, which pleases me very much. Now Reverend, carry on."

He motioned to his friend to come with him and the two calmly walked out of the church.

Jenny stood at the altar for a moment in stunned silence with everyone else. Then she came back to Luke and the Swamper.

"I can't believe anyone would ever do something so awful. Especially to a minister. And in a church. What was Curly Bill thinking?"

"Well, Luke and Jenny," said the Swamper, "that's just the way Curly Bill was. He was a wild man. Especially when he drank, which was much too often. But the funny thing was, when Bill was sober, he was a decent fellow. I guess he fell into a bad crowd when he came here, or maybe the other Cowboys just brought out the worst in him. Bill lives up near Galeyville, which is another town not too far from here. Something is about to happen there that will make Bill even more of a legend."

The next thing they knew they were sitting at a table in a saloon.

"Look at the bar," pointed the Swamper. "Bill and some of his friends are having a drink."

The saloon doors opened and a man entered.

"That's Deputy Sheriff Billy Breakenridge," said the Swamper. "Would you believe me if I told you that the deputy and Curly Bill are good friends?"

Luke and Jenny shook their heads.

"Well, believe it. And Bill is just about to prove it. See that other man over there, the one in the blue shirt?"

Luke and Jenny nodded.

"His name is Jim Wallace. He's also one of Curly Bill's friends. At least, for now."

As the deputy came up to the bar Jim Wallace looked up and yelled an insult. The saloon was noisy, so Luke and Jenny couldn't make out what he had said, but whatever it was, the deputy left, which made Bill angry. He walked up to his friend, shouting.

"You go outside, bring the deputy back in, and apologize to him."

Jim Wallace did as he was told. After all, it was never wise to argue with Curly Bill, especially when he was angry. But this time Bill was so irate that when his friend brought the deputy back he laid into him again.

"You know Wallace, you really are nothing but slime, so I've decided to kill you anyway!"

Jim Wallace must have decided it would be best to leave because he stepped outside with an angry Curly Bill following. Luke and Jenny heard them arguing outside. The Swamper stood up and motioned Luke and Jenny to follow. Just as they got outside, Jim Wallace fired his gun at Curly Bill. The bullet hit Bill in the neck and came out his right cheek.

"Whoa! I'll bet that hurt!" exclaimed Luke as he and Jenny watched Bill fall to the ground.

And just like after the shooting of Fred White, the townspeople quickly came running to the scene at the sound of gunfire. Deputy Breakenridge arrested Jim Wallace before more trouble began, while the Cowboys carried Bill off to the doctor.

"Is this how Curly Bill died?" asked Jenny.

"No," said the Swamper. "But it will start a rumor that he had. Curly Bill is one tough guy. And even though he was shot clean through the head, he makes a full recovery. This adds to the legend of Curly Bill, because after this happened, some folks believed that Curly Bill was so tough and so bad that he could even come back from the dead."

"Are you going to show us more of the things Curly Bill did?" asked Luke.

"I could, and Curly Bill certainly did a lot of things to make trouble. But we don't have time for everything since I have to get you back to that bench on Allen Street before your mother finishes her shopping. Right now we're going back to Tombstone so you can meet the real Wyatt Earp."

Chapter Six

Johnny-Behind-the-Deuce

"Mr. Swamper, I have a question," said Jenny as the three walked the streets of old Tombstone.

"What is it, Jenny?" replied the Swamper.

"If Curly Bill was an outlaw, how come he and Deputy Sheriff Billy Breakenridge were such good friends?"

The Swamper stopped.

"Well, that may take a little explaining," he said as he motioned to a nearby bench. "Let's take a seat and I'll explain it."

Luke and Jenny sat down on either side of the Swamper.

"You see, it all goes back to the Civil War," he said. "Remember me saying something about that earlier to you?"

Luke and Jenny both nodded.

"Of all the wars that have been fought since our county began, the Civil War had to be the worst. It was a war in which Americans fought other Americans, and it was all fought on American soil. But it wasn't just the soldiers fighting each other in the battlefields that made it so bad; it was the fact that the soldiers hurt civilians, too. Even women and children and old people."

The Swamper paused for a moment to take a deep breath before he continued.

"Sometimes soldiers would murder a person right in front of his or her family, or they would take people's most prized possessions away and then burn down their home. Soldiers on both sides were guilty of these kinds of wrong doings. It was a horrible, horrible war. Of course, no one in your time lived though the Civil War, and to you two it's just something you read about in your history books. But in the 1880s, most folks either lived through these things themselves, or they've heard horror stories about the war from their parents or grandparents. It's a bitter memory—not the sort of thing that folks get over very easily."

"I see," said Jenny.

The Swamper went on.

"Remember I told you that most of the Cowboys came to Arizona from Texas? You know that Texas was a Confederate state. Most of the Cowboys are Democrats, too. Well, Johnny Behan was appointed county sheriff in 1881 when Cochise County was created. He was a southerner and a Democrat, too, so naturally Curly Bill and the Cowboys approved of him."

"Aha! " said Jenny. "So you're saying that it's all about politics. Right?"

The Swamper laughed and looked at Luke.

"That's one smart sister you have there, Luke."

He glanced toward two men who were standing a few feet away.

"There are Wyatt and Virgil Earp. Let's go over and find out what they're up to."

The three walked over to the Earp brothers. As they got near they overheard Virgil.

"Wyatt, that horse of yours, Dick Naylor, needs some exercise. I'd like to take him out for a ride."

"But you know Dick Naylor's my favorite racehorse, Virgil. And I don't let just anyone ride him."

"Well, I'm not just anyone, Wyatt. I'm your older brother. And I need to go check on one of our claims out near Charleston. It's only a few miles away and I promise I'll take good care of him."

40

Wyatt thought it over for a minute.

"All right, Virgil," he said. "Just this once. But you be careful with him."

"I will, Wyatt."

Virgil stepped off the boardwalk and mounted a big, beautiful horse tied to a nearby hitching post. As they watched him ride away Jenny spoke up.

"Now why do I get the feeling that something is going to happen to Virgil on that ride?"

"You catch on quickly, Jenny. Today's the day Wyatt Earp becomes a legend. Would you like to see how it happens?" asked the Swamper.

"Sure," said Luke.

And in an instant he and his sister were standing in the desert outside of town. They saw Virgil riding Dick Naylor a few feet away from them when a man driving a buckboard wagon raced toward him. The wagon drew up to Virgil and came to a screeching halt. Not waiting for the dust to settle the panicked driver exclaimed, "Virgil, you've got to help me!"

"Why Constable McKelvey, what brings you out here? Is there trouble in Charleston? And who is this with you?"

The Swamper quickly explained that Charleston was another little mining town a few miles down the road from Tombstone. They then saw a handcuffed young man in the back of the buckboard wagon who looked very scared.

"A lynch mob is after my prisoner!" exclaimed Constable McKelvey. And sure enough, they could see men on horses coming their way.

"Lynching means a hanging," explained the Swamper, "and it's doubly bad because it happens without a trial."

"Here, I'll take him with me," said Virgil Earp.

The Constable put his prisoner on Dick Naylor, behind Virgil Earp, who then spurred the horse forward and raced back to Tombstone.

"Let's go," said the Swamper.

In a blink, they were back on the boardwalk in front of the Wells Fargo office in Tombstone, just in time to see Virgil come racing in on Dick Naylor with Constable McKelvey's prisoner. Wyatt came running out of the Wells Fargo office.

"What's going on here, Virgil? That man is a nothing but a two-bit gambler who calls himself Johnny-Behind-the-Deuce. What kind of trouble has he gotten into this time?"

"I killed a man in Charleston," said Johnny-Behind-the-Deuce as Virgil dismounted. "It was self defense. Honest! But now a mob is after me and they're going to hang me!"

While Virgil helped Johnny-Behind-the-Deuce off the horse Wyatt stepped back into the Wells Fargo office. A moment later he returned with a shotgun in his hand.

"Come with me," he said.

He led Virgil and Johnny across the street to Vogan's Bowling Alley and Saloon. The Swamper motioned to Luke and Jenny to follow the Earps into the building. They had barely stepped inside when Jenny turned to look behind her.

"Uh oh!" she exclaimed, pointing out the door.

Luke and the Swamper turned around.

"Look! A big mob is forming! And they all have guns!"

Luke and the Swamper saw a large group of armed men surrounding the door to the bowling alley. Then they heard Wyatt Earp behind them calling out.

"Virgil! Morgan! Doc Holliday! Can you come over here?"

They watched Wyatt motion to a few other men to come and help, too. He got all the men to surround Johnny-Behind-the-Deuce. Then Wyatt, still holding his shotgun, told his friends to come with him and take Johnny out onto Allen Street. As they came onto the boardwalk Wyatt addressed the crowd.

"Stand back," he ordered them. "I'm taking this prisoner to jail in Tucson so he can have a fair trial. If he's proven guilty, the law will deal with him. It's not up to any of you to judge him before all the evidence is heard."

Wyatt and his friends tried to escort Johnny-Behind-the-Deuce to a nearby livery stable. Luke, Jenny, and the Swamper walked along with them, but they didn't get very far before the mob blocked their way.

Wyatt Earp recognized one of the men in the mob.

"That's Dick Gird," explained the Swamper.

He reminded them that Dick Gird was the engineer who came with the Schieffelin brothers to start up the mines

"He's well respected in town. If Wyatt can convince him to back off, the rest of them will, too."

Wyatt Earp looked directly at Dick Gird as he spoke to the crowd in a loud voice.

"If anything should happen to my prisoner, Dick Gird will die."

Dick Gird was shocked. He swallowed hard as the color quickly drained from his face. He immediately stepped back as far as he could. Others in the crowd followed, stepping aside, making way for Wyatt to take his prisoner to the livery stable.

"That was scary!" said Jenny as they watched Wyatt take his prisoner away.

"The men in that crowd were armed and they could have easily killed Wyatt," explained the Swamper. "Yet he risked his own life to save a no-account gambler."

"Why would he do something like that?" asked Luke.

"I know why," replied Jenny. "Because you're innocent until proven guilty in a court of law, and everyone's entitled to a fair trial." She paused for a moment. "I learned that last year in my social studies class. But I really didn't understand what it meant until now."

"Then I guess this means Wyatt Earp is a hero," said Luke.

"For now, Luke," said the Swamper, "but soon things will happen that will tarnish Wyatt Earp's reputation for the remainder of his life, and beyond. Even in your time people disagree. Some people think he was a good lawman, even a hero, while others believe he was a cold-blooded murderer."

"A murderer?" asked Luke. "Who did he kill? How did that happen?"

"Well, it's a very long story. You see, Wyatt's troubles all began with a stagecoach," said the Swamper.

Chapter Seven

The Benson Stagecoach Robbery

"Welcome to state-of-the-art travel in the late 19th century, my friends," said the Swamper. "The stagecoach."

Luke and Jenny discovered they were perched on top of a stagecoach.

"Whoa!" yelled Luke as the stagecoach jerked along. They were in for a bumpy ride.

"Hang on Luke, you'll be all right," said the Swamper.

It was a dark night and it must have been cold. Luke could see patches of snow on the ground and the driver and the stagecoach guard were wearing heavy coats. It was the night of March 15th, 1881, the Swamper said. And that time of year could still have pretty cold nights. Besides being cold, he explained that stagecoach travel could be quite dangerous because of highwaymen, or robbers. And they had to be on the lookout for Indians too.

The stagecoach bumped and swayed as it made its way down the road.

"It feels sort of like riding a roller coaster, huh, Luke?" asked Jenny.

"Yeah!" said Luke with a big smile, "This is really cool!"

He looked over at the Swamper.

"So where are we, and why are we here?"

Before the Swamper could answer, Jenny spoke up.

"What's up with that?"

She was looking over the driver's head and pointing at something in the road.

Luke turned toward the road. A figure had stepped out of the shadows and onto the roadway.

"That man must be in trouble or need some help with something," his sister said. "It looks like he's going to try to flag down the stagecoach."

"Actually, that's not quite right, Jenny," said the Swamper. "This is how stagecoaches get robbed."

"Robbed?" gasped Jenny.

"I think we're about to get into trouble," said Luke.

The man in the roadway raised his arms and yelled, "Hold!"

The guard, who was a big man, responded by saying, "I hold for no one."

Several more men appeared in the roadway as the guard picked up his shotgun and took aim. Loud shots rang out in the night air and Luke and Jenny ducked for cover. Then the stagecoach suddenly lunged forward. Luke and Jenny grabbed hold of the top railings, then Luke looked up and yelled.

"Look out!"

The driver was falling forward. Jenny tried to grab him, but as she wrapped her arms across his waist he fell right through them. They watched in horror as he fell off the coach.

"Now I know we're in trouble!" shouted Luke.

The big man fired off a few more rounds at the robbers. Jenny and Luke looked back to see the poor driver lying in the roadway behind them.

Jenny looked at Luke.

"I think the guard may have got one of the bad guys, but it's too dark to tell for sure."

Luke looked forward and shouted, "So now who's driving the stage?"

Jenny turned around and saw the guard was gone too.

"We're toast!" exclaimed Luke as he and Jenny held on tight.

He knew they would have been much better off on a real

roller coaster. At least they would have been able to stop. The team of horses, frightened by the sound of the gunfire, was running away without a driver to stop them.

"Don't worry, you'll be okay," said the Swamper.

"Look Luke!" shouted Jenny as she looked down to the front of the stage.

Luke saw that the guard had climbed down from his seat and had crawled onto the wagon tongue. He looked back at Jenny.

"If he makes it, I promise I won't complain about this vacation being boring again!"

He and Jenny held their breath as they watched him reach down and somehow manage, one by one, to get the reins off the ground. Once he had all the reins back he carefully backed himself off the tongue and climbed into the driver's seat. After a few minutes of pulling back on the reins he managed to get the horses back under control.

"That was close!" exclaimed Jenny as the stagecoach finally came to a halt.

They heard some of the people inside shouting.

"He's been shot!" "He's hit!" "He's hurt real bad!"

The guard bent his head to look into the window.

"Hold on!" he exclaimed. "I'll get that man to a doctor, fast!"

And with that, he whipped the horses and the stagecoach shot forward again.

"AAAHHHH!" yelled Jenny, falling backward while the stagecoach went forward.

Luke kept hold of the rail with one hand while he held out the other hand to help his sister.

"Are you okay?" he asked.

"Uh huh," she replied as she pulled herself back up. She looked around and said, "That's funny. That should have hurt, but it didn't."

She looked at the Swamper.

"That's because we're not really here, right?"

The Swamper smiled and nodded his head.

"What happened inside the stagecoach?" asked Luke.

"One of the passengers was accidentally shot by the robbers," explained the Swamper.

"Is he going to be all right?" asked Jenny.

"No, I'm afraid he isn't."

While they sped along the road the Swamper told them that the guard was a friend of Wyatt Earp's named Bob Paul. A few minutes later they arrived in Benson. Bob Paul brought the stagecoach to a sudden halt, leapt from the stagecoach, and quickly ran to get help.

"We might as well get off here," said the Swamper. "Bob will return in a couple of minutes and he'll go back to check on his driver, Bud Philpot. He'll discover that poor Bud didn't make it either. His death will cause a great outrage among the law-abiding citizens of Tombstone. Sheriff Johnny Behan is going to form a posse to go after them, and we're going to ride along."

Chapter Eight
Luke and Jenny Ride with the Posse

Luke and Jenny suddenly found themselves standing back at the spot where the robbery had occurred. Only now it was daylight and they recognized Bob Paul, the guard, waiting nearby on a horse, as other members of the posse rode up to meet him. Luke and Jenny noticed the three Earp brothers, Wyatt, Virgil, and Morgan, were there, along with Deputy Sheriff Billy Breakenridge. Then the Swamper pointed out their friend, Bat Masterson, wearing a derby hat, along with Sheriff Behan. Another man with them that day was Marshall Williams.

"Is he a marshal, too?" asked Luke.

The Swamper laughed and explained, "No. That's his real name. Marshall Williams works for Wells Fargo, along with Wyatt Earp."

"But how can we ride with them?" asked Luke. "We don't have any horses."

"Look over there, my young friend."

They followed the Swamper's gaze and saw two other spirit people, a man and a woman, holding three horses. The horses must have been ghosts too since they also had the same eerie white glow about them that the Swamper had.

"Luke and Jenny, I'd like to introduce you to some of my friends from the Bird Cage Theatre," said the Swamper. "Meet Johnny and Marguerite. They wanted to help out, so they've brought some special horses for you to ride. Now come with me, Luke."

Luke followed the Swamper to one of the horses that Johnny was holding. Johnny was smoking a cigar, so Luke asked him if it was his cigar he'd smelled in the lobby of the Bird Cage. Johnny smiled and nodded.

"That was me. We were all watching you and Jenny and your mother in the museum, so we thought we'd have a little fun and play tag with you. We couldn't resist the fun of messing up Jenny's picture, and we all had a good laugh when your mother got upset and tried to tell you that there are no such things as ghosts."

"Johnny and his friends like to have fun with visitors to the Bird Cage," explained the Swamper, "but they mean no harm. Now, if you'll put your foot in this stirrup, I'll help you get on the horse, and Marguerite will help you with yours, Jenny."

Jenny looked over at the woman. She was very pretty with long, black hair falling over her bright red dress. She had a beautiful smile and spoke with a Spanish accent.

"Don't be nervous," she said as she helped Jenny mount. "He's a very gentle horse. Here, just hold on to the reins like this and you're all ready to go."

"Thank you," said Jenny.

"You're welcome."

"Hey Swamper," yelled Johnny, "we'll meet you over at Big Nose Kate's. A baseball game's about to start."

"I'll see you there soon," replied the Swamper as he mounted his horse. Neither Luke nor Jenny had ever ridden a horse before, but they both found that it was a lot of fun. They rode along with the posse for what seemed like a very

50

long time. The Swamper told them they were riding over several days, but that the time had been sped up for them. Finally they arrived at a ranch and everyone, including Luke and Jenny, got off their horses as a man came out to greet them.

"Mr. Redfield," said Wyatt, "we're searching for the men who robbed the Benson stage. Have you seen any of them around here?"

"Look Wyatt, over there!" shouted his brother Morgan as he pointed to another man who had spotted them and was looking for a place to hide.

Morgan chased after him and caught him in the barn as Luke and Jenny and the other posse members followed. After the man surrendered he told them his name was Luther King.

Wyatt told Johnny Behan, "You stay here with Mr. King. The rest of us are going outside to talk about what we should do next."

But as soon as Wyatt and the others left another man came in the barn and started talking to Luther King. They kept their voices low so Luke and Jenny could not make out what they were saying. But as soon as Wyatt came back in the other man bolted out.

"Behan! What have you done?" shouted Wyatt. "I told you not to let any of the Redfield brothers talk to Luther King! Don't you know that they're friends with the Cowboys?"

Wyatt began questioning Luther King, who admitted he'd held the horses for the other outlaws during the stagecoach robbery. He told Wyatt that the other men involved were Billy Leonard, Harry Head, and Jimmy Crane, and where they were camped.

"Those are all very dangerous outlaws," said the Swamper. "They won't be easy to capture. And to complicate things even more, Billy Leonard is a friend of Doc Holliday's."

Wyatt Earp looked at Johnny Behan.

"You take this man back to Tombstone. The rest of us are

going after the others. But thanks to you, no doubt Hank Redfield's already one step ahead of us, and he'll warn them that we're coming."

"What happens now?" Luke asked the Swamper.

"The Earps and the others will spend the next week and a half chasing the outlaws, then their horses will become too exhausted to keep up the chase. Virgil will send Johnny Behan a telegram asking for fresh horses, but Behan will fail to deliver them. In the end they'll come up empty-handed, and you can bet they won't be very happy when they get back to Tombstone."

"It sounds like Johnny Behan is not that smart," said Jenny.

"Or maybe he's just pretending to be dumb," said Luke.

"What do you mean?" asked Jenny.

"Well, we know that Johnny Behan is a friend of the Cowboys. And we just watched him let Hank Redfield talk to Luther King after Wyatt Earp told him not to. So I think he's secretly helping the Cowboys."

The Swamper laughed.

"You may be onto something, Luke. Would you like to test your theory?"

Luke nodded his head.

"Okay," said the Swamper. "Our next stop is the jail in Tombstone."

A moment later Luke and Jenny were in the Tombstone jail. They saw a young, blond man seated behind a desk doing paperwork. The Swamper told them the man was Harry Woods, and he was Johnny Behan's undersheriff.

"What's an undersheriff?" asked Luke.

"Like an assistant sheriff," replied the Swamper.

"Oh," said Luke.

Just then a tired-looking Wyatt Earp walked in with another man. Wyatt explained that word was out that a large group of Cowboys might be riding into town that night to try to break Luther King out of jail, and he asked Harry Woods to go back and put him in irons.

"Sure Wyatt, I'd be happy to," said Harry Woods.

Wyatt thanked him as he and the other man left, but Harry Woods stayed at his desk.

"So why didn't he go back and put Luther King in irons like he said he would?" asked Jenny.

A few minutes later another man came in, asking Harry Woods about a horse he had for sale.

"Something's not right here," said Luke.

"Come with me," said the Swamper, as he led them down to the jail cells. They arrived just in time to see Luther King step out of his cell and walk out the back door of the jail. They watched him mount a horse that was tied behind the building and ride off.

"I think you're right, Luke," said Jenny. "They're all bad cops. They really are friends with the Cowboys."

"This escape will cause a huge public outcry," said the Swamper. "Of course, Harry Woods will deny any wrongdoing. But Wyatt Earp is going to try to turn the tables in his favor. You see, Johnny Behan had promised to make Wyatt his undersheriff, but he gave the job to Harry Woods instead. So now Wyatt wants to run for sheriff in the next election. He thinks that if he can catch the robbers he'll win. He's going to make a secret deal with some of the Cowboys to make that happen. Follow me down this alley to hear them seal the deal."

Chapter Nine
Wyatt Earp's Secret Deal

"Why would any of the Cowboys want to help Wyatt Earp capture one of their friends?" asked Jenny.

"For the money," answered the Swamper. "A lot of money. Wells Fargo has put out a huge reward for the robbers— $3,600 dollars."

"Wow!" said Luke. "That would buy a lot of video games."

They followed the Swamper behind one of the saloons. Three figures stood in the darkness, then a fourth man appeared.

"Wyatt, is that you?" asked a voice.

"It's me, Ike. Who's that with you?"

"It's me, Joe Hill," said one of the other men. "And Frank McLaury is with us, too."

"Don't worry about Frank and Joe," said Ike, "I can vouch for both of them."

"All right Clanton, let's talk," replied Wyatt. "I want to make a deal with you. I want you to help me get Leonard, Head, and Crane. All you have to do is lead me to them. I'll do the rest."

Ike Clanton and the other two men laughed. Then Ike said, "Sure Wyatt, no problem. Why don't I just wave my magic wand."

All three Cowboys exploded in laughter again.

"I'm serious, Ike,"

"Okay Wyatt, so what if you are. That's a pretty tall order. What's in it for us?"

"The reward money offered by Wells Fargo."

"You don't say," said Ike. He paused for a moment. "So if the three of us collect the reward, then what's in it for you, Wyatt?"

"I take credit for capturing them. I want the glory. I intend to run for sheriff, and if you get me Leonard, Crane, and Head, I'll win for certain. Like I said, all you have to do is lead me to the outlaws, you collect the reward money, and I promise that I won't tell anyone how I got the information."

Ike, Frank, and Joe started whispering among themselves, but Luke and Jenny could not make out what they were saying. Ike spoke up.

"Look Wyatt, this may get messy. Don't get me wrong, we're all willing to take the risk, but you have to understand, these guys are dangerous. They're not just going to surrender. In fact, I doubt they can be taken alive. Will the reward be paid if they're dead?"

"I'm not sure Ike. Let me find out. I'll meet you back here tomorrow night."

"We'll be here."

"So what happens next?" asked Luke.

"We follow Wyatt," replied the Swamper.

They went back to the Wells Fargo office with Wyatt, who asked Marshall Williams for a favor.

"Would you mind sending a telegram to the office in San Francisco for me? Ask if they'll pay the reward dead or alive."

"Sure thing, Wyatt," replied Williams. "What's this all about?"

"Oh, I was just curious, that's all."

Marshall Williams sent a telegram to the Wells Fargo office in San Francisco. The reply came a short time later.

Wyatt smiled as he read the telegram. He folded it, put it in his shirt pocket, and left. He hadn't noticed how Marshall Williams was taking an interest in the telegrams going back and forth. As the door closed behind Wyatt he said out loud, "I'd sure like to know what that was all about."

"Wow! That's sort of like email," said Luke. "But how did it work? I know this was before computers or cell phones."

"You're right Luke. A telegram is sort of like email," replied the Swamper. "Back then there were telegraph wires that were mounted on poles, sort of like your modern telephone poles. These wires went to telegraph offices all over the country. Did you notice that piece of metal the operator was clicking on?"

"You mean that thing that looked like a stapler?" asked Luke.

"Yep," replied the Swamper. "He used it to tap out a code. It's called the Morse code. The different sounds he taps represent different letters of the alphabet. The sounds travel through the telegraph wires, and that's how he sends the message."

"And that clicking sound we heard…" asked Luke.

"…was the reply to the message. Then he wrote down the message, and that's what Wyatt put in his pocket." He paused. "I guess you could say that the telegraph is the great-grandfather of your modern-day email."

"Cool," said Luke.

"What now?" asked Jenny.

"We'll go back to the alley," replied the Swamper. "Remember, Wyatt said he'd meet Ike Clanton and the others there the following night. Come with me."

The three arrived in the alley just in time to see Wyatt meet up with the three Cowboys.

"I have good news, Ike," said Wyatt. "The reward will be paid, dead or alive."

"Then you have a deal, Wyatt," replied Ike Clanton.

As Wyatt walked away they heard Ike Clanton talking to

the other two Cowboys.

"You know, I think there's more to this than meets the eye. I just can't help wondering if Wyatt also wants these guys because Billy Leonard is friends with Doc Holliday, and the whole thing just doesn't look good for the Earps."

As the Cowboys left Luke and Jenny asked the Swamper if the deal worked out. Did the Cowboys lead Wyatt to the outlaws? Was he able to capture them?

"Nope," said the Swamper. "The whole thing went sour. Joe Hill thought he knew where the robbers were, but by the time he got there he discovered two of them were already dead. Turns out they weren't the only ones after the reward money. And if that wasn't bad enough, Marshall Williams' curiosity got the better of him. A short time later, he approached Ike Clanton and said he knew about the secret deal between him and Wyatt."

"But Wyatt never told anyone!" exclaimed Luke.

"I know," replied the Swamper. "It was just a lucky guess on Marshall Williams' part. But Ike Clanton took a big chance in making this deal with Wyatt. He really was trying to do the right thing, even if it was for the wrong reasons."

"You mean he should have been willing to help Wyatt catch the bad guys because of what they did, not because of the reward money," said Jenny.

"That's right," said the Swamper. "But if other Cowboys, like Johnny Ringo or Curly Bill, knew what Ike and his buddies were up to, they'd have killed them. So we still have to give Ike and the others credit for being willing to take the risk. Ike Clanton thought Wyatt had betrayed him, and now he was angry and scared. Not only was he afraid the other Cowboys would find out, he was worried about Doc Holliday too. He worried about what would happen to him if Doc were to find out that he was willing to help in planning the killing of his friend, Billy Leonard."

"It sounds like Marshall Williams stirred up a lot of trouble," said Jenny, "even if he didn't mean to."

"Indeed, he did," said the Swamper. "And you're right, Jenny, he may not have meant to, but he did nonetheless. You know, trust is a funny thing. It can take a long time to build, and it can be easily broken."

"But Wyatt didn't do anything wrong," said Luke.

"I know that," replied the Swamper, "and you know that. But Wyatt can't prove that he didn't. That's why you should never stick your nose into other people's business or meddle into their personal affairs. Nothing good ever comes from it, and Marshall Williams' actions will end up costing other people their lives."

Luke and Jenny listened to the Swamper's words and thought about what he had to say as they walked down the streets of old Tombstone.

Chapter Ten
Fire! Fire!

As Luke, Jenny, and the Swamper strolled down the streets of old Tombstone they noticed that most of the people they passed looked hot and uncomfortable and the sky was bright with summer heat.

"Where are we?" asked Luke.

The Swamper chuckled.

"The real question is, 'When are we?' It's a very hot day in the month of June, 1881."

"How did everyone stay cool?" asked Jenny.

"They didn't," replied the Swamper. "The air conditioning that you take for granted in your time is a long way off. We didn't even have the electricity to power a fan. During the summers it was hot and people would sweat. A lot. Our clothes would get soaked with sweat and that's how we got cool. Sort of."

"Eeew," said Jenny. "That sounds icky. I'll bet you had to take a lot of showers."

Again the Swamper laughed.

"Jenny, we didn't have modern plumbing either. If we wanted to take a bath we had to fill the bathtub with water that we poured out of pitchers. That is, if we even had a bathtub. Not everyone did. So we didn't bathe much either."

Jenny wrinkled her nose again.

"You're right, Jenny," said the Swamper, "People weren't as clean or comfortable back in my time. We didn't eat as well as you do either, because we didn't have much fresh fruit or vegetables. That's probably why we didn't live as long as people do in your day. Back then, if you made it to your 50s, you were pretty old. In your time people in their 50s are still middle-aged. So the next time your mother gives you a hard time about not eating your vegetables, remember she's not doing it to be mean. She's doing it because she wants you to grow up strong and healthy so you'll live a long time."

Luke thought about it for a moment.

"So did you do anything to beat the heat?"

"Well, just like in your day, we loved ice cream, and we ate a lot of it in the summers. Of course, we didn't have all the fancy flavors that you have," said the Swamper as he winked at Luke. "And we built our houses a little differently. We put windows on each side of the room, right across from each other. That way, when we opened them, the breeze would blow right through. And sometimes folks would hang wet sheets across the open windows to help cool the air down when it blew through. That was as close as we could come to air conditioning."

As they walked down the boardwalk the doors of the Arcade Saloon opened in front of them. They stopped to watch two men rolling a large wooden barrel onto the boardwalk.

"What's up with that?" asked Luke.

"They're trying to dispose of a barrel of whiskey that's gone bad," explained the Swamper.

The men stopped and set the barrel upright. One man looked at the other.

"Let's measure how much is in here before we pour it all out."

"All right," replied his companion.

They carefully unplugged the barrel. One of the men

placed a gauge inside, only to have it slip out of his hands.

"Dang it all!" he exclaimed.

"Here, let me help!" came a voice from inside the saloon

Out rushed a bartender, eager to help. But the bartender had a lit cigar in his mouth, and as he bent down and got close to the whiskey fumes there was a bright flash of light and a very loud BOOM.

Luke and Jenny threw their arms across their faces and ducked. They felt the ground shake beneath their feet at the sound of the explosion. A fire had started and the flames were spreading down the boardwalk.

The Swamper led them off the boardwalk and into the street where they watched the fire spread to nearby buildings.

"Don't worry," he said. "The smoke and flames can't hurt you since you're not really here."

People rushed up and down the street yelling, "Fire! Fire!"

Luke and Jenny tried their best to keep out of the way. But at times so many people were running by that a few ran right through them. It didn't hurt, but it seemed strange nonetheless.

The fire spread quickly, fueled by the dry wood on the buildings. Then a hot wind started to blow.

"The heat of the fire creates its own wind," said the Swamper. "That's what's meant by the word 'firestorm.'"

A group of people formed a line and passed buckets of water, but their attempt to put out the fire was useless. It had grown too big and was spreading too fast. Shop owners and bankers put their goods and money in the street to save them from burning. Others with axes chopped up the boardwalks and porches to try to keep the fire from spreading even further. But it kept growing. Finally vacant lots and alleys stopped it, then it burned itself out. The Swamper told them that the fire burned for several hours and that in the end it destroyed several square blocks of the city. He also said the

61

people were lucky. Only one man was seriously hurt when he fell from a balcony, but he healed just fine.

"Look, Jenny!" exclaimed Luke.

Tents had been erected where the burned out buildings had stood, and the town was back in business.

"Tombstone people are a tough lot," said the Swamper. "It would take more than this to get them down. The town was rebuilt within a month."

Indeed everything had been rebuilt. And as they passed a boarding house they heard the sound of a man and woman loudly arguing inside. The Swamper sighed.

"There they go again. Doc Holliday and Big Nose Kate have, what you would call in your time, a very dysfunctional relationship."

"You mean they fight a lot?" asked Jenny.

"They sure do," said the Swamper. "They're known for having some spectacular fights."

"Then why doesn't she leave him?" asked Luke.

The Swamper shrugged his shoulders.

"I'm not much into love or romance. But I hear folks say that despite the fact that they fight like a couple of cats, they really do love one another—in their own strange way."

At that moment the door to the boarding house burst open and Kate ran out. She turned and shook her fist at the door.

"You're going to be a very sorry man, Doc Holliday!"

A voice behind them called out.

"Why Miss Elder, what seems to be the problem?"

Luke and Jenny turned to see Sheriff Johnny Behan standing behind them. He walked up to Kate.

"There, there Kate, why don't you come with me and tell me all about it."

As Kate and Johnny walked away the Swamper said, "It's now July, 1881 and we're about to see some real fireworks."

Chapter Eleven
Big Nose Kate

"Please step into my office, Kate," said Sheriff Behan as he opened the door. Luke, Jenny, and the Swamper followed them inside.

"Have a seat," he said, pointing to a chair across from his desk.

Kate took a seat as Luke, Jenny, and the Swamper sat down on a nearby bench. Although Kate was still a young woman, she looked sad and tired beyond her years. The simple blue and white plaid dress she wore made her look plain. And Jenny noticed too that it looked like Kate was getting a black eye and that she may have been crying. Sheriff Behan got a bottle of whiskey and poured a glass for Kate.

"There you are, my dear. This will help calm your nerves," he said, handing her the glass.

As Kate sipped her drink the sheriff sat behind his desk and took out a pen and paper to take notes. Dipping his pen into a bottle of ink, he started asking Kate some questions.

"So, Miss Elder. Is that really your name?"

"No sir. It's Haroney. Mary Katherine Haroney."

"I see," said Sheriff Behan. "And I hear that you were born in Hungary."

"Yes sir, that's right," replied Kate. "We came to Mexico in the early 1860s. My father was a doctor for the Emperor Maximilian. But we didn't stay in Mexico for very long.

We came to the United States—to Iowa. Then both of my parents died. That was in 1865. I was only 15 years old. I ran away from my guardian and was a stowaway on a Mississippi riverboat."

"My, my, Kate. You certainly had an interesting youth," said Sheriff Behan. "So what happened after that?"

"I met and married a man by the name of Silas Melvin," replied Kate. Her eyes grew misty as a long-forgotten memory crossed her mind.

"I wonder what's the matter with her," said Jenny.

"I've heard talk that she had a baby when she was married to Silas, but that the baby died," said the Swamper.

"Oh," said Jenny, "I see. That's really sad." She thought about it for a moment. "Did she ever have more children?"

"Nope," said the Swamper, shaking his head.

Kate took a few more swallows of her drink.

"The marriage didn't last. Later, I met Wyatt through his sister-in-law, Bessie. You know, she's James Earp's wife."

"Yes, I know who Bessie Earp is," said Behan. He stood up and opened the whiskey bottle. "Here, let me refresh your drink," he said as he refilled Kate's glass.

"Back then, I thought Wyatt was my knight in shining armor." She sighed and smiled, then the smiled faded and she looked very sad. "But Wyatt didn't feel the same, and he broke up with me." She took another sip of her drink. "Later on, I met Wyatt's friend, Doc Holliday. He and I have been together ever since."

"Yes, I know," said Sheriff Behan. "I've heard a rather interesting story about the two of you that happened in 1877 in the town of Griffin, Texas. Would you like to tell me about that, Kate?"

"You bet I would!" said Kate. "You know that Doc is a gambling man. One day he was playing poker with a man named Ed Bailey. But Ed Bailey was a cheater! And he and Doc got into it. Ed Bailey had a gun! So what was Doc supposed to do? He had to defend himself! Doc had a knife.

And he took his knife and reached across the table and —"

"Yes, Kate, I know the rest of the story. Doc made sure that Ed Bailey would never have the chance to cheat at cards again. But Doc got arrested for that, didn't he?"

"Yes, he did. And they might have hung him for it, too!"

"But you saw to it that didn't happen, didn't you Kate?"

"Yes, sir." She paused and took another sip of her drink. "Doc was my man, and I had to save him. So do you know what I did?"

She paused and looked around the room for a moment,. Then she leaned forward and looked Sheriff Behan in the eye.

"I set fire to the hotel where they were holding Doc, and then I shoved a pistol into the guard's stomach and I made sure that he let Doc go. Then we made our getaway!"

"On stolen horses," muttered Behan under his breath.

"We made our way around the West," said Kate.

She paused for a moment as if she were remembering something, then she took a few more sips of her drink and started to laugh.

"One time, when we were living in Las Vegas, New Mexico, some lawmen showed up at our house. They wanted to arrest Doc. But I wasn't going to let that happen. So there I was, in my nightgown on the front porch, pointing a pistol at the lawmen. I told them that if they wanted something, they could come and get it." She started laughing again. "It wasn't long after that when Wyatt sent for Doc to come to Tombstone."

"So here you are. Now what is it that you wanted to tell me, Kate?" asked Behan.

She took a few more sips of her drink.

"Doc Holliday was in on the Benson stagecoach robbery."

"What!" exclaimed Behan. "Are you sure?"

"Of course I'm sure. I wouldn't be here if I wasn't."

She paused and finished her drink. Johnny Behan picked up the whiskey bottle and quickly poured her another one.

"One of the robbers, Billy Leonard, is a friend of Doc's. And do you want to know something else, Sheriff?"

"What is that, Miss Kate?"

Kate picked up her drink as she leaned back in her chair.

"Doc Holliday visited Billy Leonard the morning of the robbery."

While Kate sat back and finished her drink Johnny Behan shuffled papers on his desk and quickly wrote notes. Then he pushed a paper across the desk to Kate.

"I want you to sign this statement for me, Kate," said Behan. "It says exactly what you said."

Kate took his pen and signed the paper.

"What happens next?" asked Luke.

"Well, the next day, after she sobered up, Kate went back to Sheriff Behan and tried to recant her story," said the Swamper.

"Recant?" asked Luke.

"Yep. That means she said that she was wrong. She claimed that Sheriff Behan had gotten her drunk and she didn't know what she was saying."

"So was she able to recant her story?" asked Luke.

"Not really. Behan arrested Doc Holliday for being a part of the robbery. But in the end the case was thrown out of court for lack of evidence. But Kate's actions end up creating all kinds of trouble, not only between her and Doc, but also because they start rumors all over town about Doc and the Earps being involved in the robbery."

"Was Doc involved?" asked Luke.

"You know, I don't think anyone other than Doc Holliday himself really knows for sure. Even in your time, people don't agree. Some say Doc was in on it; some say he wasn't."

"Can we ask Doc ourselves?" asked Luke.

The Swamper laughed.

"That would be bad manners, Luke. If Doc decides he wants you to know, he'll tell you."

"I don't know if I like Kate or not," said Jenny. "It sounds like she did some awful things. And why doesn't she use her real name?"

"You must remember that Kate lived in a time when the world didn't have much to offer women," explained the Swamper. "You're lucky, Jenny. When you grow up you can go to college and get a job doing whatever you like, or you can get married and stay home and take care of your children if you want to. In Kate's time women didn't have those choices. Very few women went to college. Mostly they depended on their fathers or husbands to take care of them. But Kate lost her father when she was still a young girl, and Doc just wasn't the marrying kind. So Kate had to do whatever she could to get by.

"She also lived during a time when women were supposed to be very prim and proper. You just heard her tell the sheriff about some of the things she did that weren't very ladylike. So that's why she goes by different names. If she makes a bad name for herself somewhere she can move and start over with a different name.

"Now imagine if Kate had been able to live in your time. She would have had more choices and her life would have turned out a whole lot better."

"What became of her?" asked Jenny.

The Swamper explained that years later, after Doc died of his Consumption, Kate married a man named Cummings, but that marriage didn't last either. She never married again. Later on in life she found work as a housekeeper and spent her last days living in Prescott, Arizona, where she died in 1940 at the age of 89. She is buried in Prescott as Mary K. Cummings.

"Are she and Doc back together now?" asked Jenny.

"They were, the last I heard. Despite everything, she and Doc were made for one another."

The Swamper led them back outside. It was nighttime again.

"Come this way," he said. "Things in Tombstone have gone from bad to worse. And we're about to have a showdown."

Chapter Twelve
The Showdown Begins

"Where are we off to now, Mr. Swamper?" asked Jenny.

She, Luke, and the Swamper were strolling down the streets of Tombstone and enjoying the sounds of laughter and piano music coming from the many saloons. It appeared to be a very cold night since they could see the breath of the people they passed on the boardwalk.

"Things are about to come to a head, as you say in your time," said the Swamper. "It's been five months since Marshall Williams told Ike Clanton he knew of his secret plan to help Wyatt Earp catch the stagecoach robbers. Ike's been living in fear ever since. He's terrified of what would happen to him if Curly Bill or Johnny Ringo were to hear of it. And lawlessness is becoming more of a problem in Tombstone. Johnny Behan just can't seem to get the job done."

He stopped in front of the Alhambra Saloon.

"We're going to eavesdrop while Wyatt and his brother Morgan have lunch."

While Jenny passed through the swinging doors of the saloon she echoed, "Lunch? But it's dark outside. What time is it anyway?"

"Oh, it's probably about 11:30 or so at night," replied the Swamper.

"At night?" asked Jenny. "Isn't that the wrong time for lunch?"

"In my time, Tombstone never sleeps. I suppose in a town like this you can have lunch anytime you want. Here, let's take a seat near the bar so you can see what's going on."

Wyatt and his brother seamed to be having a pleasant meal together.

"Look over there," said the Swamper, pointing to a man with curly blond hair and a blond mustache and beard. "That's Ike Clanton. It was too dark in that alley for you to get a good look at him. And look who else just walked in—Doc Holliday himself."

Luke and Jenny turned to see a pale, thin man with a mustache walk in.

"That's Doc Holliday?" asked Luke.

"Yep," said the Swamper.

"But he's so thin! In the movies he's always this great big guy," said Luke.

"Why are people so afraid of him?" asked Jenny. "He doesn't look like he could hurt a fly."

"Don't let looks deceive you, Jenny," said the Swamper. "It's because Doc is so frail and sick that he's become so tough and mean."

Doc Holliday had spotted Ike Clanton. He got a cold, angry look in his eye as he walked up to Ike and shouted insults at him, calling Ike a liar, among other things.

Wyatt Earp, who was still eating his lunch, turned to his brother.

"Morgan, since you're Virgil's deputy, I think you'd better go over there and take care of that."

Morgan slipped off his stool and approached Doc and Ike. He led Doc outside, but Ike followed, and the two kept arguing.

"Let's go," said the Swamper.

He motioned Luke and Jenny to follow. Luke and Jenny saw Wyatt step outside just as Virgil arrived.

"All right, that's enough out of both of you!" Virgil shouted. "Stop your quarreling now or I'll take both of you to jail!"

Doc and Ike separated, each going his own way. After they left Morgan said, "Good night, Virgil, Wyatt. I'm heading home. I'll see you two tomorrow."

As Morgan walked away Virgil told Wyatt, "I'm off to the Occidental Saloon."

"And I've got to get back to the Eagle Brewery," said Wyatt. "I've got a faro game going there."

"Faro?" asked Luke.

"It's a card game. Sort of like poker, "explained the Swamper. "It was very popular in Tombstone."

"Oh," said Luke.

They watched as the two Earp brothers walked away.

"Whew!" said Jenny. "That was close."

"Oh, it's not over, Jenny," said the Swamper. "In fact, it's only just begun. Look over there." He pointed down the street to the Eagle Brewery. "Come with me."

As Luke, Jenny, and the Swamper approached the Eagle Brewery they saw Wyatt step back outside. Ike Clanton came up to him.

"Wyatt, would you mind taking a walk with me? I want to talk to you about something."

"Sure, Ike," replied Wyatt, "but I can't go very far. I still have a faro game going."

"I understand," said Ike.

Luke, Jenny, and the Swamper walked behind Wyatt and Ike like shadows as they walked down Allen Street. Ike told Wyatt that when Doc Holliday approached him in the saloon he said that all this fighting talk had gone on for too long, and that it was time to put an end to it and have it out, man to man, once and for all.

"I told him I wasn't interested in having a fight," Ike said. "But he walked off saying he'd be after me in the morning. So I decided to go over to the Oriental Saloon to have a drink. He followed me in, with his six-shooter, and again told me not to think that he wouldn't be after me in the morning. So

Wyatt, I'll tell you what. I've had enough of this! I'm ready to fight him now."

"Come on, Ike, I really don't think he wants to fight you."

"Why do I not believe that?" asked Jenny.

"You're right Jenny. Wyatt is just trying to calm Ike down," said the Swamper.

Just then another man came up to speak to Wyatt. As he and Ike parted company the Swamper told Luke and Jenny they would walk around with Ike for a bit.

"It sounds like he really doesn't want to fight," said Luke.

"Maybe not," said the Swamper, "but you can bet he's really ticked off. I guess I would be too, if someone were insulting me and making threats against me like Doc Holliday just did. After all, it's human nature to want to defend ourselves. Now you're about to see something really unbelievable, considering everything that just happened. Look!"

They watched Ike Clanton walk into the Occidental Saloon and sit down at a poker table with Virgil Earp, Johnny Behan, and two other men. The Swamper pointed to one of the men.

"I don't know who that other fellow is, but that's Tom McLaury sitting right there. Remember Tom and his brother Frank are part of the Cowboy gang, and Frank was one of the two men Ike had with him when they made the secret deal with Wyatt. They'll spend the rest of the night drinking and playing poker, but tomorrow, they'll meet again, and with a tragic outcome!"

Chapter Thirteen
Ike Clanton Searches for the Earp Brothers

It seemed as if Luke, Jenny, and the Swamper had been watching the poker game at the Occidental Saloon for only a few minutes when Luke glanced at the doors and noticed the sun was rising. About that time Virgil Earp looked at his pocket watch.

"Gentlemen, it's seven o'clock. I'm going home to my wife to get some rest."

The men got up from the table. As Virgil started out the door Ike called out.

"You can give your brothers and Doc Holliday a message for me. Tell them Ike Clanton says they'll have a fight!"

Virgil Earp ignored Ike Clanton as he walked out the bar and headed home.

The Swamper told Luke and Jenny they would be keeping an eye on Ike Clanton. Along with playing poker, they knew that Ike Clanton had been drinking all night. It was plain to see, as he stumbled and wound his way up Allen Street, that he was very drunk. A short time later he wandered into another saloon and told the bartender he was looking for the Earps and Doc Holliday, and that as soon as he found them there would be a fight. The bartender, as well as Luke and Jenny, noticed that Ike had a pistol tucked in the waistband of his pants. The bartender urged Ike to go on home, but Ike would hear nothing of it.

"I thought he said he didn't want to fight," said Jenny.

"He must have changed his mind," said Luke.

They followed Ike into the next saloon, where he again told anyone who was listening that he was looking for the Earps and Doc Holliday. He said that the night before Doc had insulted him, but he was not heeled at the time. Now that he was heeled, as soon as he found them, there would be a fight. Again the bartenders told Ike to go home and sleep it off.

"What does he mean by 'being heeled'?" asked Luke.

"'Being heeled' means being armed," explained the Swamper.

As they followed Ike from saloon to saloon the Swamper explained that word about Ike was starting to get around town and that a few of the bartenders had gone to both Wyatt and Virgil's homes to warn them, but both men had remained in bed, saying it was just Ike's idle talk.

"I don't think it's idle talk at all," said Jenny. "He looks like he means it. And look! Now he has a rifle, too."

They followed Ike to C.S. Fly's Photo Studio and Boarding House, where Doc and Kate lived. Ike knocked on the door and when Mrs. Fly answered, he told her that he was looking for Doc Holliday and that there was going to be a fight. She saw the rifle and appeared shaken up. The Swamper told Luke and Jenny that Mrs. Fly would warn Doc and Kate, and that Doc would soon be out looking for Ike.

They continued to walk the streets behind Ike, who kept telling anyone and everyone he saw that he was looking for the Earps and that they would soon have a fight.

"I wish there was something we could do," said Jenny. "I feel so helpless, not being able to warn the Earps."

"Don't worry, Jenny," said the Swamper, "The Earps are pretty good at taking care of themselves. Look over there."

They saw Virgil and Morgan Earp across the road and watched as Virgil came up behind Ike and grabbed the rifle.

Ike struggled and reached for his pistol. Virgil grabbed his six-shooter and struck Ike across the head, knocking him to the ground. He reached down to grab Ike's pistol.

"I hear you've been looking all over town for me, Ike. Well, here I am."

"You're a lucky man, Marshal Earp," growled Ike. "If I'd seen you a second sooner, I would've killed you!"

"I'm arresting you for carrying firearms within Tombstone city limits," said Virgil. "And I'm taking you to Judge Wallace right now."

Luke, Jenny, and the Swamper followed the Earps and Ike Clanton to the courtroom, but the judge was not there. Virgil left Ike with Morgan while he went to find the judge. While Ike dabbed his bleeding forehead with his handkerchief Morgan taunted him. He challenged him to a fight right then and there. As the two argued other people in the courtroom ducked for cover.

"Geeze!" exclaimed Luke. He looked at Morgan and asked, "Why do you want to egg him on like that?"

"I'm not sure I like Morgan Earp either," said Jenny. "Now that Ike is unarmed, Morgan is standing there acting like he's some stuck-up Mr. Big Stuff."

She looked at her brother.

"Good thing he can't hear us, huh, Luke?"

"Well, Morgan is known for having a bad temper," said the Swamper. "I suppose that's why not everyone likes him."

Wyatt came in and joined the argument. Finally Virgil came back with the judge. Ike Clanton was fined $25.00, but not put in jail. Virgil told Ike he would take his weapons to the Grand Hotel. They had all just left the courthouse when they came upon Tom McLaury, who said that he had come to check on Ike.

"Are you heeled?" Wyatt asked Tom.

"Come on Wyatt, we're friends. I've never done anything against you or your brothers." He paused and then said, "But I'll tell you what. If you ever decide you want to fight, I'll have one with you. Anytime, anywhere."

"Then we'll have one now!"

Wyatt slapped Tom across the face with one hand while he reached for his pistol with the other. He slammed it across Tom's head twice, smearing blood across his face.

Once again, Jenny decided she'd had enough. She walked up to Wyatt.

"You jerk! You just beat up a man who told you he was your friend! Why, you're no better than Curly Bill! And I don't think I like you anymore, either!"

"Calm down, Jenny," said the Swamper. "He can't hear you. And remember, he feels just as angry, and just as scared, as Ike Clanton does. How would you feel if an armed man was marching up and down the street threatening to shoot both you and your brother?"

She thought about it for a moment.

"I would feel scared and angry. And I would want to do something about it."

"Exactly," said the Swamper. "The Earps are angry because Ike has been running around town waving a gun and threatening them. And Ike thinks Wyatt betrayed him, and he thinks Doc Holliday plans to kill him, so now he's going to fight back. He's gotten everyone else all riled up too. This is what happens to people when fear and mistrust take over. They begin doubting their friends and anyone else around them. Then they get scared and begin thinking that everyone's out to get them, so they may decide they're going to get them first. And what may have started as a simple misunderstanding begins to take on a life of its own. It's not a good thing. In fact, this is how wars get started, too. Common sense goes out the window and, unless cooler heads can step in, people—sometimes innocent people—end up getting hurt, or worse."

"What happens now?" asked Luke as Wyatt walked away from Tom McLaury, who was still shaking.

"See that man who just walked up to Ike? That's his

friend, Billy Claiborne. He's going to take Ike to the doctor, and we're going to go take a walk to the Grand Hotel."

Chapter Fourteen
Tensions Mount

Jenny scanned the lobby of the Grand Hotel.

"Oh, Mr. Swamper. I see what you meant when you said this place was grand."

She stopped to take in the room with its elegant furnishings.

"It's so beautiful!"

She looked at Luke.

"I can't believe this is the same Big Nose Kate's Saloon where we just had lunch. It looks so different."

She looked back at the Swamper.

"So this really was your home?"

"Yep, indeed it was," said the Swamper, with a look of pride on his face. "And I took good care of it, too."

"Can you take me downstairs and show me your secret tunnel?" asked Luke.

"Luke!" exclaimed Jenny, "That's not a very nice thing to say!"

The Swamper laughed.

"Sorry son, but a man's entitled to keep a few secrets. And I'll never tell anyone about my hidden treasure. Not even you."

He smiled again at Luke.

"Besides, it's so much fun watching all you modern folks wonder about it."

They went into the saloon. Luke looked around.

"Look who's sitting at that table over there, Jenny. It's Doc Holliday."

Two men entered the room and walked up to the bar.

"How are you two today?" Doc Holliday politely asked.

The men gave him a slight nod then ordered their drinks. The Swamper told Luke and Jenny that the two men were Billy Clanton, Ike's younger brother, and Frank McLaury, Tom's brother.

"I didn't recognize Mr. McLaury," said Jenny.

It was so dark the night they had their secret meeting with Wyatt that she and Luke had not been able to get a good look at him.

Another man sauntered in. Billy and Frank looked up.

"Hey, would you like to join us for a drink?"

"Frank, can I talk to you about something?" asked their friend.

He had a worried look on his face, so Frank stepped aside to talk to him. Luke and Jenny heard him tell Frank about his brother just having been pistol whipped by Wyatt Earp.

"Now why would Wyatt go and do something like that?' asked Frank. "That doesn't make any sense at all."

His friend shrugged his shoulders and said he didn't know.

Frank looked toward Billy.

"We'd better go find our brothers. Some sort of trouble's brewing, and we'd best leave town."

Luke, Jenny, and the Swamper followed Frank and Billy out of the hotel. As they walked down Allen Street the Swamper asked, "Have you seen why some days stand out in history?"

"What do you mean?" asked Jenny.

"On certain days something happens that will never, ever be forgotten. Like the Ides of March. That was the day

Julius Caesar was murdered in the Roman Senate," said the Swamper. "Today is Wednesday, October 26, 1881. And history will record this as another day that will never be forgotten."

As they walked along they came across Billy Claiborne.

"Have you seen Ike?" asked Billy Clanton. "I want to get him home."

"Yes I have," replied Billy Claiborne. "I just got back from taking him to the doctor. Ike's been stirring up a lot of trouble around town. That is, until Virgil Earp gave him a pretty good whack on the head."

Billy Clanton and Frank McLaury looked at one anther. Then they quickly turned the corner and went into a building.

"Why are they going in there?" asked Luke. The building was Spangenberg's Gun Shop. "If they don't want a fight, then why don't they just leave?"

"I don't know," said the Swamper. "Probably because they're scared of the Earps with what just happened to Ike and Tom. But you're right, Luke, their coming in here is certainly going to make a bad situation much worse."

Luke, Jenny, and the Swamper went into the gun shop. Tom McLaury was already there. As the three men loaded bullets into their gun belts Luke and Jenny heard a strange sound. A horse had come untied from the hitching post and had climbed onto the boardwalk. It was starting to come into the gun shop. Luke and Jenny started to laugh.

"Look Jenny," said Luke, "the horse wants to buy some bullets, too."

Luke walked up to the horse and started to grab the reins, but they went right through his hands, just like when he tried to grab the barrel of Curly Bill's gun. He looked at the Swamper.

"Come on! You mean if I move this horse, I would change history?"

"Yep," replied the Swamper. "Turn around and look

behind you."

Luke turned around to see Wyatt Earp holding the horse's bit and starting to back him out. Then Frank and Billy came to the door.

"I'm sorry, Wyatt," said Frank as he took the bridle.

Wyatt curtly replied, "You'd better get this horse off the boardwalk."

"Sure Wyatt, no problem," said Frank as he pushed his horse back off the boardwalk and retied him to the hitching post.

"Wyatt sure didn't look too happy," said Jenny. She and Luke saw that Wyatt was carefully watching the men stock up on bullets.

Ike Clanton walked in with his bandaged head.

"Mr. Spangenberg," he said, "I'd like to look at a pistol."

"Sorry Ike, not today," replied the shop owner. "You've been making too much trouble around here today. Besides, your head's still bleeding. Come back tomorrow when you're feeling better."

"Let's go," said one of the Cowboys as they headed out the door.

"We're going, too," said the Swamper. "Let's find out what the Earps are up to."

Chapter Fifteen

The Earp Brothers On the March

"Hurry Virgil!" exclaimed a man running up to Virgil on the street. He pointed to Spangenberg's Gun Shop.

"Wyatt's down there and the Cowboys will surely kill him!"

Luke, Jenny, and the Swamper watched Virgil go into the Wells Fargo office. He stepped back out a moment later with a shotgun in his hand. As he walked along the street townspeople ran up to warn him about the Cowboys, begging him to disarm them. Then Johnny Behan came up to him.

"Virgil, what on earth is going on around here? I overslept this morning and was in the barbershop when someone rushed in and told me trouble was brewing."

"It's those Cowboys," said Virgil. "They're in town and just itching for a fight. Perhaps you should disarm them."

"Now Virgil, you know that I'm more a tax collector than a lawman," replied Behan. "And besides, my deputies are all out of town tracking down escaped prisoners."

"Is this guy good for anything?" asked Jenny.

"Then maybe we should go together," said Virgil.

But Johnny Behan quickly left, explaining that he might have a better chance of disarming the Cowboys if he went alone.

"Sure," said Jenny, "they're all your buddies."

In the meantime several other men approached Virgil, telling him the Cowboys were over by the O.K. Corral. Virgil told everyone that as long as the Cowboys stayed there and were leaving town he wasn't going to bother them. But if they came back into town, he would take away their arms, since it would be against the law to carry them within the city limits.

Virgil met up with his brothers Wyatt and Morgan and his friend Doc Holliday. While they talked things over Virgil handed his shotgun to Doc Holliday and asked if he would hide it under his long, gray overcoat. He explained that the gun was attracting too much attention. Doc took the shotgun and hid it while handing his walking stick to Virgil. The four men walked the streets together.

"He must have changed his mind about not bothering them if they stayed at the O.K. Corral," said Luke. "I've seen this scene before in the movies, and I know what happens next."

"From what I hear, it was Wyatt who talked Virgil into going and disarming the Cowboys," said the Swamper. "And you're right, Luke. Virgil should have stayed with his plan to let the Cowboys leave town."

Chapter Sixteen
The Shoot-out on Fremont Street

Luke, Jenny, and the Swamper headed to Fremont Street. As they approached the O.K. Corral they saw Billy Clanton and Billy Claiborne pass through the back of the corral and into a vacant lot that stood between Fly's Photo Studio and Boarding House and another house.

"What are they doing there?" asked Luke, "Why don't they just leave?"

Just then Ike Clanton walked up and joined his brother and the other Billy in the vacant lot.

"Maybe they're waiting there to meet their friends," said Jenny. "Look, there they are."

She pointed to the two McLaury brothers who were standing in front of a nearby butcher shop. Then Johnny Behan appeared and asked Frank McLaury for his weapons.

"Sorry, Sheriff, I can't do that," replied Frank, "But don't worry. I don't plan to cause you any trouble. In fact, I think you should disarm the Earps instead of me."

"Come with me. Let's all have a talk," said Behan as he led the two McLaurys into the vacant lot where the others were waiting. They were still talking when they looked up and saw the Earp brothers and Doc Holliday marching toward them.

"Wait here," said Sheriff Behan, "I'll see what they want."

As Johnny Behan turned and approached the Earps one of the Cowboys shouted, "Don't worry, Johnny. We're not going to cause any trouble."

The Earps met Johnny Behan near the entrance to the O.K. Corral.

"Gentlemen, I'm the sheriff of this county, and I'm not going to allow any trouble."

The Earps' response was to keep walking. Johnny Behan ran behind them yelling, "Stop!"

Virgil stopped and turned to Johnny Behan.

"I've come to disarm the Cowboys."

"I've already disarmed them," shouted Behan.

As the Earps and Doc Holliday walked toward the vacant lot Sheriff Behan ran after them shouting, "Stop! Stop!"

"This reminds me of that time you missed the school bus, Luke," said Jenny.

"Very funny!" responded her brother.

"Look! Did you see that?" asked Jenny.

"What?" replied Luke.

"Virgil had been holding the walking stick in his left hand."

"So?"

"Didn't you notice that when Behan said he'd already disarmed the Cowboys, Virgil switched hands? He put the gun on the left side of his waistband, and put the walking stick in his right hand. I noticed that Virgil is right-handed, so since he put the gun on his left side, he probably believes the Cowboys are disarmed."

The five Cowboys were standing in the small vacant lot when the Earps and Doc Holliday arrived. Sheriff Behan stopped near the door of Fly's Boarding House. Billy Claiborne stepped aside and stood next to Behan as the other four men stepped farther back into the lot. That's when the Earps discovered that the Cowboys had not been disarmed after all.

Luke and Jenny sensed the tension in the air. They stopped at the entrance to the vacant lot and decided not to go any farther.

"This is it!" said Luke.

Jenny reached over and pulled her brother aside. Even though she knew they really couldn't get hurt, she still wanted them to be as far out of the way as they could.

Virgil Earp raised the walking stick up in his right hand.

"Throw up your hands, boys. I want your guns!"

"I don't want a fight," answered Billy Clanton, as Tom McLaury opened his overcoat, letting the Earps know he was unarmed.

Both Frank McLaury and Billy Clanton started reaching for their six-shooters.

"Maybe they really meant to hand their guns over," said Luke.

The air was quiet and still. The silence was broken with the sound of a click-click—the quiet sound of a gun being cocked. But in the quiet chill of that October afternoon, it seemed as loud as a clap of thunder.

"No! I don't want that!" shouted Virgil.

But it was too late and the sounds of gunfire suddenly burst out. Both Luke and Jenny dropped to the ground and ducked for cover. Two gunshots sounded like they had come from the direction of the Earp party. There was a pause, and then the air exploded with more gunfire.

Luke peered up and saw Sheriff Behan pushing Billy Claiborne into the door of Fly's Boarding House. Then he saw Tom McLaury behind his horse, reaching for his rifle, which was in the saddle scabbard, or holster. But as the shots began firing the noise scared his horse and it jumped out of his reach.

Doc Holliday lifted the shotgun from underneath his coat, walked around the horse, and came up behind Tom. He opened fire. The blast from the shotgun was so strong that it sent Tom staggering into the street.

"But he's unarmed!" shouted Luke.

As the shots kept firing Jenny saw Billy Clanton take a shot in his chest, then his wrist, and another in the stomach. He slumped back against the building, switched gun hands, and kept firing as he slid down the side of the wall.

Luke looked around to see Ike Clanton lunge at Wyatt Earp. Wyatt grabbed him by the shirt and saw that Ike was not armed.

"The fighting has begun!" he roared. "Either get to fighting or get out!"

Jenny heard the shouting too and looked over. Ike Clanton pushed Wyatt aside as he ran into the photo gallery. He ran out the back of the building and down the street.

"Look at that! He just ran off and left his brother behind to get killed! What a coward!" shouted Jenny to her brother.

"He's unarmed," said Luke. "If he stays, he'll get killed, too!"

They looked back and saw Virgil Earp being shot in the leg and going down. His brother Morgan was firing at Billy Clanton, who by now was sitting in the dirt and shooting with his pistol balanced on his knee. Morgan took a bullet to the shoulder.

"I'm hit!"

He fell and tried to get back up but it looked like he may have tripped on something, because he stumbled back to the ground.

In the meantime Doc Holliday tossed the shotgun away and was drawing his pistol.

"Look over there, Jenny!" shouted Luke as he pointed to Frank McLaury, who was using his horse as a shield and backing onto Fremont Street.

Doc fired another shot and the horse broke free and ran, leaving a badly injured Frank slumped down all alone on the street.

Doc went after him as Frank staggered to his feet and

raised his gun.

"I've got you now!" Frank shouted.

"Fire away!" yelled Holliday in return. "You're a daisy if you do!"

Frank McLaury took aim and fired, grazing the frail dentist on the hip.

"Weren't expecting that, were you?" shouted Luke.

As Frank struggled across the street both Morgan Earp and Doc Holliday opened fire, with one bullet hitting Frank in the chest, the other in the head. Frank McLaury was done for. He fell into the street, never to rise again.

Then came silence as a haze of gray gun smoke lifted in the air. Luke and Jenny sat up.

"Are you all right, Jenny?" Luke asked his sister.

She looked pretty shook up. Instead of speaking she pointed at a man running out of Fly's Boarding House toward Billy Clanton, who was still sitting in the dirt. He was trying to reload his pistol when the man reached down and took the gun from him. Dazed, Jenny shook her head.

"How could something this horrible have happened?"

The Swamper knelt down.

"I don't really know what the answer is. This is what happens when people stop thinking clearly and let their fears take over. I guess that fear brings out the worst in all of us."

A crowd of people gathered at the scene.

"What happens now?" asked Luke.

"Frank has already passed away," said the Swamper. "The people will take Tom and Billy Clanton to nearby houses and try to get help for them, but we all know that they won't make it. Whether they were good men or bad men, it's a very sad day in Tombstone."

Chapter Seventeen
A Funeral in Tombstone

The sign in the undertaker's window read, MURDERED ON THE STREETS OF TOMBSTONE. Luke, Jenny, and the Swamper stopped to look at the three bodies, dressed in their Sunday best, lying in black caskets beautifully trimmed with silver. The coffins had been propped up behind the window so that folks passing by could get a good close look.

"They look so calm and peaceful," said Jenny, "almost as if they were just taking a nap and will wake up soon. It's hard to believe that they had such a bad ending."

"How's everyone taking it?" asked Luke.

"About as well as can be expected," said the Swamper.

He explained that right after the shooting most folks in town saw the Earps and Doc Holliday as heroes. Even newspapers in places like San Francisco hailed the Earps as brave men who had rid Tombstone of dangerous outlaws. Everyone knew that the Clantons and McLaurys had been cattle rustlers who ran with a bad crowd.

"What happened to Ike?" asked Luke.

"He got arrested right after he fled the gunfight," the Swamper explained. "And he's still in jail, but he'll be out again very soon. His other brother, Phin, came to town and spent the night at the jail with Ike."

"And what about the Earps?" asked Jenny.

"They're at home, recovering from their wounds," said the Swamper. "Johnny Behan paid them and their wives a visit the night of the gunfight, and they all ended up having a rather bad argument."

"About what?" asked Luke.

"Well, the Earps weren't exactly happy to see him, which I think would be expected, considering what just happened. And the fact that there has always been bad blood between them certainly doesn't help."

Luke looked around. He noticed that the boardwalk was becoming crowded. Very crowded. Then he turned back to the undertaker's window.

"Look!" he exclaimed, "They're gone!"

Jenny and the Swamper turned to see that the window display was empty.

"What's that?" asked Jenny. "I think I hear a band playing,"

Turning to face the street she and her brother saw the funeral procession go by. A brass band played somber funeral music. It was followed by Billy Clanton's casket on a horse-drawn hearse.

"Look at that, Luke. That looks just like the hearse we saw in the Bird Cage Theatre."

Following Billy Clanton's casket was another horse-drawn hearse carrying the bodies of the two McLaury brothers. It was followed by a wagon carrying Ike and Phin Clanton and many, many people on foot. Hundreds of people lined both sides of the street up and down the boardwalks for several blocks.

"I didn't realize that the Clantons and McLaurys were so popular," said Jenny.

"I don't think it's that," said the Swamper. "A lot of folks just have a morbid curiosity, that's all. The gunfight was a big story in newspapers all over the county and this funeral will be a big story too. Some of the business people here will begin to worry about what other folks think of Tombstone.

If too many of them get the wrong idea, it could be bad for business."

Luke and Jenny looked back at Allen Street and noticed the crowds were gone and everything seemed to be back to normal. The Swamper explained that a few days had passed, and that the coroner's inquest had just been held.

"What's a 'coroner's inquest'?" asked Luke.

"Oh, that's a legal term," explained the Swamper, "It's what happens when there's a death that's not from natural causes. The coroner needs to determine whether or not foul play was involved. It's done in your time as well."

"And in this case?" asked Jenny.

"The coroner simply stated that the McLaury brothers and Billy Clanton died of gunshot wounds inflicted by the Earp Brothers and Doc Holliday."

"Well, duh!" said Luke.

Then they noticed Ike Clanton passing by with a look of fierce determination in his eye.

"That doesn't look good," said Jenny as she, Luke, and the Swamper caught up to Ike to see what kind of trouble he was up to now.

They followed him to the courthouse. Upon entering he said, "I'm here to file murder charges against Virgil, Wyatt, and Morgan Earp, and Doc Holliday."

Chapter Eighteen
The Hearing

"Hear ye. Hear ye. This court is now in session. The Honorable Wells Spicer presiding."

The judge entered the courtroom and took his seat at the bench. He addressed the onlookers.

"You may be seated."

Luke, Jenny, and the Swamper stood at the very back of the courtroom since every seat had been taken. The judge continued.

"The matter before us is a preliminary hearing to determine if the defendants are to be bound for trial. I understand all the defendants have posted bail. Do you have legal counsel?"

A man rose and said, "Yes, your Honor. I am Tom Fitch. I'm representing the defendants, Virgil, Morgan, and Wyatt Earp, and John Henry Holliday."

"Thank you, counselor, you may be seated," said Judge Spicer. "And for the prosecution?"

"Lyttleton Price, your Honor, District Attorney for Cochise County. I will be assisted by Ben Goodrich."

He went on to mention the names of several other lawyers who would be working with him.

"That's a lot of lawyers," said Jenny. "It doesn't look good for the Earps. How long will this go on?"

"It will last about a month," said the Swamper. "We won't need to stay for all of it, but we'll listen in on some of the more important testimony."

The first witness called was Billy Allen, who testified that he had followed the Earps on their march to Fremont Street, and that someone in their party had yelled, "You've been looking for a fight!"

He went on to testify that Tom McLaury had thrown open his coat and yelled, "I don't want to fight!" and then Billy Clanton held his empty hands out telling the Earps that he didn't want to fight either, but that the Earps began to gun them down anyway. He also told the court that Doc Holliday and the Earps fired the first shots. The defense questioned him about his past, trying to attack his credibility, but the court would not allow it. Then Allen left the stand.

The next witness called was Johnny Behan. He told the court how he had tried to prevent the Earps from entering the vacant lot, but that they had brushed past him. He also told of hearing Billy Clanton say he did not want to fight, and that Tom McLaury had indeed opened his coat saying that he was not armed. He went on to say that the Earp party had fired the first shots, and while he couldn't be certain, he thought that Doc Holliday fired the first shot.

The Swamper told Luke and Jenny that because Johnny Behan was a well-liked sheriff his testimony would begin to cast serious doubt about the Earps and public opinion would start turning against them.

"By the time Behan leaves the stand, the prosecution will have the upper hand."

After Behan more and more witnesses also testified that Tom McLaury had thrown his coat open, and that he and Billy Clanton had said they did not want to fight. They all agreed that the Earps and Doc Holliday had fired first and that they had all gotten several rounds fired before the Cowboys were able to start fighting back. Then Luke and Jenny noticed that another attorney had joined the prosecution team. The Swamper told them that the attorney had come all the way from Texas, and that his name was William McLaury. He was Frank and Tom McLaury's brother. And as more witnesses were called the prosecution team, along with William McLaury, was able to convince the judge that Doc Holliday and Wyatt Earp should be held in jail for the duration of the hearing.

The Swamper noticed that Luke had gotten a very concerned look on his face.

"What's the matter?" he asked.

"I was just thinking," said Luke.

"What about?"

"I think I saw Doc Holliday reaching for his shotgun and Morgan Earp reaching for his gun just before I heard that clicking sound. And Morgan Earp and Doc Holliday were standing behind Virgil, and I know Virgil Earp was looking at the Cowboys so he wouldn't have seen them."

He paused for a moment.

"Mr. Swamper, I can't be certain, but I'm wondering if either Doc Holliday or Morgan Earp were the ones cocking their guns. I think that's what Virgil Earp heard just before he shouted 'I don't want that!' Maybe Doc Holliday or Morgan Earp really is the one to blame for starting it. I don't think either one meant to, but I think one of them did."

The Swamper leaned back against the wall.

"You know Luke, you may be onto something. But you see, people have been debating about who did what for over a century now, and the only thing we do know is that no one will ever know for certain. Even the people who were there can't agree on exactly what happened or who fired the first shot."

"I know someone who might know," said Jenny. "When the shooting stopped, I looked up, and I thought I saw Big Nose Kate looking out of the upper story window of the boarding house. Why don't they ask her?"

"Unfortunately, Kate isn't a believable witness. She's known as a drunk and a liar. So even if she did come forward, who would believe her?" said the Swamper.

While the three were talking other witnesses were called to the stand and the prosecution's case grew stronger with each one.

Billy Claiborne testified that Doc Holliday fired the first shot, Morgan Earp the second. By the time Ike Clanton was called it seamed certain that the Earps and Holliday would be held over for trial.

Ike began his testimony by telling the story of the argument he had with Doc Holliday the night before and how Morgan Earp had taunted him in the courtroom the following day. His story backed up what the other witnesses had testified to at the beginning of the shoot-out. Then things began to go wrong for the prosecution as he told a rather interesting story of grabbing hold of Wyatt after the shooting began and pushing him through the photo gallery door.

"That's not what I saw!" exclaimed Jenny. "He may have pushed by Wyatt as he ran by, but I didn't see him push Wyatt into the photo gallery."

Ike went on to say that he then exited through the back of the photo gallery so he could retrieve his wagon and horse team and leave town.

One of the prosecuting attorneys asked Ike if he had ever, at any time, threatened either the Earps or Doc Holliday.

"No, sir," replied Ike, "I've never threatened any of the Earps or Doc Holliday."

"Yeah, right," said Luke.

Then came time for the defense to cross-examine Mr. Clanton. It wasn't long before Ike admitted that he actually had used threatening language against the Earps in one of the saloons on the morning of the gunfight. Then the defense began questioning him about the deal he had made with Wyatt to capture Leonard, Head, and Crane—the three men who had tried to rob the Benson stagecoach and killed Bud Philpot.

"I asked him why he was so anxious to capture these fellows," Ike answered. "He said his business was such that he couldn't afford to capture them, that he would have to kill them or else leave the country, and that he and his brother Morgan had piped off the money from the stagecoach to Doc

Holliday and William Leonard."

"Piped off?" asked Luke.

"He's saying that Wyatt and Morgan stole the money and gave it to Doc," explained the Swamper.

"No way!" exclaimed Luke. "Jenny and I were there. We saw it! The robbers never got the money off the stagecoach!"

The defense continued questioning Ike about the deal, and Ike kept denying that a deal was ever made. He even denied it when he was presented with the telegram that Wyatt received from Wells Fargo explaining that the reward would still be paid if the robbers were killed.

"Liar!" exclaimed Jenny.

"I know why he's lying," said Luke.

"Why?"

"Because he's still scared of someone like Curly Bill finding out. He has to deny it. If he admits it, then he gets killed."

"Good point," said Jenny.

Ike went on telling more and more tales of how the Earps had told him that they had secretly been involved in the stagecoach robbery, and that he had been keeping the Earps' secret all this time, but Luke and Jenny weren't buying it.

"Would anyone believe that the Earps could have confided something like that to Ike Clanton?" asked Jenny. "I didn' think he was that close of a friend."

"That's a very good observation, Jenny," said the Swamper, "and a lot of folks will come to the same conclusion. The prosecution had a strong case until Ike took the stand, but this testimony is too unbelievable, and it's really hurt their case. The defense will now present its side, but it's already over for the prosecution."

The defense began its case by calling Wyatt Earp to the stand. Wyatt told stories of confrontations between the lawmen and the Cowboys, and said that he had never leaked the secret deal between himself and Clanton. He explained that it had instead leaked out when Marshall Williams guessed their involvement. He went on telling of more threats and confrontations between himself and the Clantons, McLaurys, and their Cowboy friends.

He then said that once inside the vacant lot Billy Clanton had pointed his gun at him, but that he, Wyatt, had aimed his gun at Frank McLaury, and that the first two shots were fired almost at the same time. One by him, and the other by Billy Clanton. He said that he did not draw his gun until after Billy Clanton and Frank McLaury drew theirs, and he admitted shooting Frank in the stomach. He also told of pushing Ike Clanton away because he was unarmed.

"I see what you mean about not everyone agreeing about what happened and who did what when," said Jenny. "I guess it all happened so fast."

The questioning continued.

Wyatt said, "If Tom McLaury was unarmed, I didn't know it. I believe he was armed and fired two shots at our party before Holliday, who had a shotgun, fired at and killed him."

He said that all the threats Ike Clanton and Frank and Tom McLaury had made led him to think that the three men had planned to murder him, his brothers, and Doc Holliday. Therefore, he was justified in shooting them. He went to the vacant lot that day with his brothers to disarm them and it was not his intention to fight unless it was in the line of duty, or in self-defense, or to protect the lives of his brothers or Doc Holliday. Before leaving the stand Wyatt denied that he was ever involved in the Benson stagecoach robbery.

"Now the defense will start tearing down the prosecution's case," explained the Swamper. "More witnesses will be called to the stand, including Virgil Earp, and they will cast doubt on the earlier testimony. Then it will be up to Judge Spicer to decide. Meanwhile, let's step outside and get some fresh air."

Chapter Nineteen
The Verdict

"Thank you, Johnny. I appreciate it," said the woman as she stepped aboard the stagecoach.

"You're welcome, Kate. Anytime," replied the man who helped her board. He tipped his hat and walked away.

Jenny stood in stunned disbelief.

"Was that Big Nose Kate who just got on that stagecoach?"

"Yep," said the Swamper.

"But the hearing isn't over yet! Her boyfriend's still in trouble. And she's leaving town?" asked Jenny.

"Yep. Rather odd, isn't it?" said the Swamper. "And what's even funnier is that the man who helped her is Johnny Ringo. He loaned her the money for the fare. And Ringo and Doc hate each other with a passion that I've never before seen."

"Kate's friends with her boyfriend's worst enemy?" asked Jenny.

"That's right," replied the Swamper.

"That's bizarre," said Jenny. "If it was my boyfriend, I wouldn't leave. I wonder if Kate is hiding something."

"Maybe it's one of those 'on again off again' relationships that people in your time seem to have," suggested the Swamper.

"Or maybe it's because she saw that Doc and Morgan really did shoot first, and she doesn't want to have to testify against him," said Jenny. "He's probably still upset with her for talking to Johnny Behan."

"That could be, I suppose," said the Swamper, "and if that is the case, then maybe she's wise to leave."

He paused for a moment.

"But we'll have to let Doc and Kate worry about it. We have to get back to the courtroom. The verdict is about to be read.

Judge Wells Spicer looked tired when he entered his courtroom on the afternoon of November 30, 1881. He began by telling the court that he would be reading a statement, and that his decision would come after the statement was read.

It was a very long statement. He explained that he only considered the facts that were agreed on by both sides or were established by consistent testimony by the witnesses. He was not going to consider anything that had been disputed, such as whether or not Doc Holliday or the Earps had been involved in the stagecoach robbery. He explained that he believed that Ike Clanton had been making threats against the Earps on the day of the gunfight, and that Virgil Earp was performing his duty by arresting him for violating the city ordinance against carrying firearms.

The judge read on, rehashing the events of that fateful day and the testimony of some of the witnesses. He stated that the Earps were officers of the law who were charged with disarming known criminals who had refused to be disarmed, and that he believed the Earps had acted in self-defense.

"I cannot resist the conclusion that the defendants were fully justified in committing these homicides—that it was a necessary act done in the discharge of an official duty."

He then read the verdict.

"The evidence taken before me in this case would not, in my judgment, warrant a conviction of the defendants by a trial jury of any offense whatsoever."

"In other words," said the Swamper, "The Earps and Doc Holliday are free to go. They won't be held for trial. And while the Earps won their case, they lost in the court of public opinion," said the Swamper.

"What does that mean?" asked Luke.

"It means that too many people have been left with too many doubts. You know Luke, even in your time, some people still believe that the Earps were secretly involved with the stagecoach robbery."

As the people filed out of the courtroom, the Swamper asked Luke and Jenny.

"So, what do you two think?"

"I'm not sure," said Jenny. "At first I sided with the Earps. But now, after hearing other witnesses and thinking about what I saw, I'm not sure. Maybe they could have handled it differently."

"I think everyone's to blame," said Luke. "Too many things went wrong that day for it to be one person's fault."

A voice behind them said, "You're right, Luke. There's enough blame to go around for everyone, and all of us who were there that day bear some responsibility for what happened. Johnny Behan and I probably bear most of the responsibility because we were the lawmen in charge."

Luke and Jenny turned around to see Virgil Earp, but this time he had the same white glow about him as the Swamper. They knew that Virgil was addressing them as a spirit person.

"You know, people in your time like to say that hindsight is twenty-twenty," said Virgil. "I've thought a lot about what I could have done differently that day. What if I had stuck to my decision not to go over to the O.K. Corral? What if the Cowboys had left town sooner? What if the judge had put Ike in jail that day? What if the Cowboys had not gone to Spangenberg's Gun shop and stocked up on ammunition? But you know what? We could have done everything differently, and we still might have had a similar outcome on a different day. What happened happened, and as much as all of us would like to, we can't go back and change the past. We have to learn to live with the consequences of our actions and move on with our lives."

Virgil looked over at the Swamper.

"Good seeing you again."

"You too," replied the Swamper.

Virgil tipped his hat as he slowly faded away.

"Is there more?" asked Luke. "I figured that since the court case is over we'd reached the end of the story."

"A few more stories remain," said the Swamper. "You may have thought that the Earps' troubles were over, but that's not the case at all. In fact, the real trouble for Wyatt and his brothers has hardly begun."

Chapter Twenty

The Cowboys Seek Revenge

"'Twas three nights after Christmas, and all through the town, all is not well," said the Swamper. Luke and Jenny giggled at his attempt to be poetic.

He explained that since the time of the verdict things had gone from bad to worse in the town of Tombstone. Because the hearing had left so many unanswered questions many people now believed that the Earps really had been involved in the stagecoach robbery, and they did not agree with Judge Spicer's decision. Those who had once supported the Earp brothers now thought they should have gone to trial. There had even been an attempt to assassinate the mayor, John Clum, who was a friend of the Earps, during what was made to look like a stagecoach robbery.

"Was he okay?" asked Luke.

"Yep," said the Swamper. "However, the mayor is also the editor of one of our town newspapers, The Epitaph. That paper supports the Earps. But our other town newspaper, The Nugget, opposes the Earps. The two papers are having a war of words, which is making things even worse around here."

The Cowboys had been keeping a room upstairs at the Grand Hotel. The window of that room had a good view of the street and they removed the shutters to make it even better.

"Look up there," he said, pointing to the window. "You can see for yourselves."

"Oh, yeah," said Luke, "and I can see someone looking out of that window, too." He paused and said, "That's creepy. Good thing they can't see us, huh, Jenny?"

The Swamper told them that the Earps had been getting so many death threats that they and their families moved out of their homes and into the Cosmopolitan Hotel.

"Look, Luke," said Jenny. "Over there. It's the Bird Cage Theater."

"Yep," said the Swamper. "It just opened a few days ago."

They walked over to the Bird Cage and heard music and laughter coming from inside. A man in a top hat passed them and went inside. As he entered they could see that the bar and the stage were in one big room. Instead of the dark and dreary museum they had seen earlier, this was bright and cheery. Many men crowded around tables playing cards while a small group of women in saloon girl dresses danced on the stage.

"Can we go in?" asked Luke.

"No, not tonight. It's not a place for youngsters like you," said the Swamper.

"Aw, come on!" replied Luke.

The Swamper ignored Luke's protests and kept walking down the street with Jenny. Luke waited a moment, then ran to catch up with them just as they were approaching a dark, open building that looked like it was still under construction. In the darkness it looked especially scary.

"That looks creepy," remarked Jenny.

As they walked by they heard creaking sounds. Jenny suddenly stopped. She looked at her brother.

"I thought I just heard someone walking around in there. Did you just hear something?"

"Yeah," said Luke, not sure what to do next.

Looking across the street to the Oriental Saloon he saw Virgil Earp standing in front of it. He appeared to be looking at something in the building as well. Luke tapped his sister on her shoulder and pointed.

"Look! Over there. It's Virgil Earp."

They heard more creaking sounds.

Jenny whirled around at the sound of the noise. Peering into the darkness she could just make out the shape of a double-barreled shotgun pointed at her brother and her.

"Luke, look out!"

She pulled her brother back with one arm and tried to push the shotgun away with the other. But as had happened so many times before, her hand went right through the barrel. The gun went off with a sound like thunder. And not one gun, but several. The loud noises boomed into the night air. She shrieked, covering her ears and jumping backwards. When the shooting stopped she gave the Swamper a strong look.

"It's okay, Jenny," said the Swamper. "Those blasts could've gone right through you, and you still wouldn't have gotten hurt."

"Jenny! Look over there!" exclaimed Luke. "Virgil's been hit!"

But he was too late. Jenny had taken off after the shooters. Luke ran over to Virgil.

"Are you okay, Mr. Earp?" he asked, forgetting for the moment that Virgil could not hear him. He yelled to the Swamper.

"He's alive!"

Virgil managed to get back on his feet. Luke wanted so much to help him up, but since he couldn't, he walked along with him as he staggered back into the Oriental Saloon. He could see that Virgil had been hit in his back and left arm. As people in the saloon came to help him to his room he heard Jenny running up behind him.

"I think there were two or three men," she said, trying to

catch her breath, "but I couldn't tell in the dark. Some of the men in town tried chasing them, too, but they got away."

She asked the Swamper, "What happened to Virgil? Will he be all right?"

The Swamper explained that while Virgil was seriously injured he would survive. However it would take a few months for him to recover, and even then, he was never going to be the same again.

"The bone in Virgil's upper left arm was shattered," he explained, "and the doctors are going to have to take most of the bone out. He'll lose the use of that arm."

"So who did it?" asked Luke.

"That's a good question, Luke," said the Swamper as they stepped back onto Allen Street. "No one knows exactly who for sure, but we all have our suspicions. Unfortunately, as Jenny just told you, the shooters got away. However the next day Wyatt will find Ike Clanton's hat in the back of that building. Wyatt will also telegraph the U.S. marshal in Phoenix asking to be appointed deputy U.S. marshal to replace his brother."

"Does he become the deputy marshal?" asked Luke.

"Yep, he does," said the Swamper. "But he'll get a lot of criticism for it. Too many folks around here have lost faith in the Earps."

"So what about Ike Clanton?" asked Jenny. "Will he finally go to jail this time?"

"That's the amazing thing, Jenny," replied the Swamper. "Wyatt will get an arrest warrant for the Clanton brothers— Ike and Phin—and another outlaw by the name of Pony Deal. And several posses will go out after them."

He explained that in the months after the shoot-out on Fremont Street the people in Tombstone became more and more nervous. The outlaws became bolder and bolder and crimes like stagecoach robberies became more and more common. It seemed like posses were riding in and out of town everyday, which made people feel even more ill at ease.

Adding fuel to the fire were the local politicians who were arguing back and forth while the two town newspapers also kept people on edge with their ongoing war of words.

"Then what happened?" asked Luke.

"The Clanton brothers eventually got arrested for the attempted murder of Virgil Earp. And it looked like the prosecution had a strong case against them," said the Swamper, "but then the defense called in several witnesses, including Constable McKelvey, from Charleston."

"I remember him," said Luke. "He was the one who had Johnny-Behind-the-Deuce in his wagon. He asked Virgil to help him."

"Unfortunately, this time Constable McKelvey wasn't much help to the Earps. He testified that Ike Clanton was in Charleston the night Virgil was shot."

"So why was his hat found in the building the next day?" asked Jenny.

"Ike testified that he'd lost his hat before the shooting and he had no idea how it ended up there," replied the Swamper.

"I'll bet," said Luke.

"So then what happened?" asked Jenny. "Did they go to jail?"

"The case against the Clantons was dropped," said the Swamper. "The hat was circumstantial evidence. And you can't convict someone on circumstantial evidence. You need hard proof. No eyewitnesses ever came forward claiming to see Ike Clanton fleeing from the scene."

"I know," said Jenny, "I ran after them, but I couldn't tell for sure who they were. It was too dark."

"People will always have their suspicions of who it was, but the real identity of who tried to kill Virgil Earp will always be a mystery," said the Swamper.

"At least Virgil lived," said Jenny. "So what happened next? Did the Earps leave Tombstone?"

"Not then, but they would have been much better off if

they had," said the Swamper. "For now, Wyatt and Morgan have been joined by their younger brother, Warren, and they seem to always be out on patrol, while Virgil stays in bed recovering from his wounds. Unfortunately, something even worse is about to happen to them."

Chapter Twenty-One
The Death of Morgan Earp

Luke, Jenny, and the Swamper were enjoying a quiet evening stroll down Fremont Street, across from the vacant lot where the fatal shoot-out between the Earps and the Cowboys had taken place. It was a stormy night and the wind was howling, which made it look even spookier.

"How long has it been now?" asked Jenny, tilting her head toward the empty lot.

"Let's see," said the Swamper. "It's now the middle of March—the 18th, in fact—and it's a Saturday night."

Walking past Schieffelin Hall the three saw a sign for a play that night called "Stolen Kisses." They heard the sound of footsteps behind them. When they turned around they saw Wyatt Earp stop in front of the theater.

"I wonder what he's doing here?" asked Jenny.

The theater doors opened and people began pouring outside.

"It looks like the play has just ended," said the Swamper.

Wyatt Earp was still standing behind them when his brother Morgan came out of the theater and walked up to greet him.

"See Wyatt, I told you. Everything's fine. You worry too much."

"Someone has to have some horse sense around here," said Wyatt. "Like I told you before, I have a bad feeling about tonight. Not only did I got a message from Johnny Ringo that he wouldn't be a part of any trouble, I've also seen a few other Cowboys hanging around town today. I came here to meet you so I can walk you back to the hotel."

"But things have been pretty quiet around here for the past few weeks," replied Morgan. "I'm beginning to think the worst may be over. And Virgil is doing much better too. Hey older brother, I'm a big boy now. I can take care of myself."

"But you'll always be my baby brother. Besides, I promised Louisa that I'd look after you while she's in California visiting her folks."

"Wives," said Morgan. "They worry too much too."

The two brothers began walking, with Luke, Jenny, and the Swamper close behind.

"The night is still young Wyatt, and I've been cooped up in that hotel too long…" Morgan paused for a moment. "Since you're here with me, why don't we stop along the way at Campbell & Hatch's and shoot a few games of pool? After that I promise not to argue with you anymore. We'll go back to the hotel. All right?"

Wyatt knew it was useless to try to argue.

"Okay, Morg, but just for a little while."

By then they had walked back to Allen Street. As they came up to Campbell & Hatch's Luke said to the Swamper, "Hey, this is where we were sitting when we met you."

"And it's where you're still sitting, Luke," replied the Swamper. "Do you remember me telling you I would be bringing you back here to show you something?"

"Yep," answered Luke.

"Well, this is it. Come on inside with me."

Inside they noticed Morgan and Wyatt enjoying a game of pool and a few other men playing with them. They stood near the pool table and watched Morgan bend over to line up his shot. No one thought anything of the fact that his back was toward the back door of the saloon.

BANG. BANG.

The sound of two gunshots and breaking glass suddenly erupted. Luke, Jenny and everyone else in the room ducked for cover. Morgan Earp slid off the pool table and onto the floor right beside Jenny. But something didn't look quite right. Morgan Earp wasn't moving as others started to get back on their feet. She reached over and tried to touch his shoulder.

"Are you hurt?" she asked.

Jenny screamed and jumped to her feet when she noticed a pool of blood forming around him. Morgan had been shot in the back.

"NOOOO! Morgan!" screamed Wyatt.

Wyatt wasn't hurt, but he was in great distress over his wounded brother. The other men gathered around to help and they heard someone say that the bullet had passed through Morgan's body. Then they saw that another man, who had been standing next to Morgan, had been hit in the leg by the same bullet. The other man's injuries were not serious. Morgan, however, was carried into another room while doctors were summoned.

In the meantime Luke ran to the back of the room to see who fired the shots. Two other men had run back as well, going past him as they flew out the back door and raced down the alley. A few moments later they returned, saying the shooters had fled and it was too dark to see who it was.

Three doctors soon arrived but there wasn't much they or anyone could do, other than try to keep Morgan as comfortable as possible. The bullet had gone all the way through his body and there was no way that he would recover. Other members of the Earp family came, including Morgan's faithful dog. With each gasp of breath Morgan looked paler and weaker. Everyone knew that he would not be around much longer. Members of the Earp family wept, as did Luke and Jenny.

She reached back into her backpack, taking out the

handkerchief Fred White had loaned her. She looked at Luke and the Swamper.

"I'm sorry I said such bad things about him that day at the courthouse when he was picking on Ike Clanton. I never wanted anything like this to happen to him."

"It's all right, Jenny," said the Swamper. "Morgan knows you meant him no harm. He would be the first to admit that he's a bit cocky."

Jenny grew silent again as she and the others watched Morgan struggle to cling to life. Finally he lifted his hand, motioning Wyatt to come closer. As Wyatt sat holding his dying brother's hand Morgan whispered something in his ear. Then he took one final, raspy breath. With his exhale his entire body went limp and the light went out of his eyes. Morgan Earp would breathe no more. Then his dog whimpered, as if it too knew that its beloved owner was gone.

Luke and Jenny sat silently as the Earps left and Morgan's body was taken away. After everyone left Jenny finally asked, "Did they ever find out who did this?"

"No," said the Swamper. "To this day, no one knows who killed Morgan Earp."

Chapter Twenty-Two
A Hero Becomes a Villain

Luke stood up and walked to the door. The sun was now shining and he could hear the sound of a church bell tolling.

"Look, Jenny! Come over here," he called to his sister.

She came, and the Swamper followed. The three stepped outside to watch Morgan's funeral procession pass by.

"They're going to the train station in Benson," said the Swamper. "James, the oldest brother, will take Morgan's body to California where the rest of the Earp family lives. He'll be buried there."

"Will James come back to Tombstone?" asked Luke.

"No," replied the Swamper. "The Earps' time in Tombstone is nearly over. When Wyatt returns from Benson he'll make arrangements for Virgil and his wife, Allie, to leave too. It's become much too dangerous for Virgil to stay here any longer."

Luke and Jenny suddenly found themselves at a railroad platform.

"Where are we now?" asked Luke.

"Back in Contention," said the Swamper.

A voice next to them said, "Wyatt, are you sure I can't stay and help?"

Luke and Jenny turned to see Virgil Earp, with his arm in a sling, talking to Wyatt.

"I'm all right, Virgil," said a weary looking Wyatt, "but

I have a tough job to do. I have to hunt down whoever murdered Morg. And I can't do it if I have to worry about you." He paused for a moment, then said, "You've done your job here, Virgil. It's time for you and Allie to head on home to California."

A man came up to Wyatt and told him that he'd just heard there might be trouble when the train reached Tucson.

"Ike Clanton, Frank Stilwell, and some of the other Cowboys have been hanging around the train station there. They're probably waiting to ambush Virgil."

"That's it then," said Wyatt.

He called his brother Warren, Doc Holliday, and his other friends over. He told them what was happening.

"We're going along with Virgil to Tucson," he said.

"We might as well get on the train, too," said the Swamper. Luke and Jenny eagerly got on board. They looked around the plush railroad car as they watched the other passengers board. Soon the train was off.

"This is totally cool!" exclaimed Luke, "It's even more awesome than the train ride at Disneyland would have been."

They had only been traveling for a short time when evening fell and the train pulled into the Tucson station

Jenny looked out the window and said, "This is Tucson?"

The Swamper nodded his head.

"Yep. This is Tucson."

"But it's just a little dinky town," said Jenny. "I can't believe this is the same city we drove through this morning on our way to Tombstone. There were a lot of cars on the freeway and skyscrapers in the city too."

"I suppose a town would change a bit after a 120 or so years, Jenny," said the Swamper. "We've reached our stop— this is where we get off."

As they stepped onto the platform the Swamper told them that the Earps had gone to a nearby hotel for dinner but they would soon return. Luke and Jenny walked around the railroad yard looking at the village of little adobe buildings that made up Tucson, but it was dark and hard to see. Soon Virgil and Allie and the others were back. Virgil and Allie went back on board the train while the others kept an eye out, looking for troublemakers.

"Look over there!" exclaimed Luke

He was pointing to a flatcar on a track next to Virgil and Allie's train. He could make out two figures lying on the flatcar and it looked like they had rifles or shotguns pointing at the railcar window where Virgil and his wife were sitting.

"I see them!" yelled Jenny. Then she looked around. "Look Luke, Wyatt just spotted them too! Here he comes! And it looks like he's carrying a shotgun!"

Wyatt Earp came around the platform and ran at the two men. Luke, Jenny, and the Swamper followed close behind.

"Jenny!" shouted Luke, "I can't tell for sure, but I think one of those men might be Ike Clanton!"

The two men saw Wyatt coming and fled. As they ran through the railroad yard one man fell behind and Wyatt quickly caught up to him.

"Frank Stilwell!" he shouted, "I might have know it was you who murdered my brother!"

Luke and Jenny could see that Frank was shaking.

"He must have dropped his gun," said Jenny, "I don't think he's armed anymore."

Frank lifted one trembling hand to grab the barrel of Wyatt's shotgun while he raised his other hand to try to protect his face.

"No!" he shouted. "Please, Wyatt, don't kill me! I'm begging–"

But before he could finish his sentence Wyatt raised up the shotgun and fired both barrels, point blank, into Frank Stilwell. He fell to the ground, dead.

"Whoa!" shouted Luke. "I guess he showed him, huh?"

Wyatt turned and ran after the other man who was

fleeing across a set of tracks and then behind some moving cars, forcing Wyatt to stop and wait for the train to pass. Once it was gone, so was the other would-be assassin.

Wyatt went back to Virgil and Allie's train, which was just about to pull away from the platform. He looked through the window at Virgil and shouted, "One for Morgan!"

While the trained pulled away the Swamper asked, "Now Luke, what's wrong with this picture?"

"I don't understand," replied Luke.

"A minute ago, when Wyatt killed Frank Stilwell, you said that Wyatt showed him."

"Yeah," said Luke, "what about it? Frank Stilwell killed Morgan, so Wyatt got even and killed him."

"That's the point, Luke," said the Swamper.

"I think I know what the Swamper's trying to say," said Jenny. She looked at her brother and said, "It's because we can't be totally certain that it really was Frank Stilwell who killed Morgan, because the shooters got away and no one got a good look at them."

"That's part of the answer, Jenny," said the Swamper.

"Remember what you two saw in Tombstone? It would have happened about a year or so ago, in my time. Remember when Virgil took Wyatt's horse, Dick Naylor, out for a ride, and Constable McKelvey came up to him with Johnny-Behind-the-Deuce in the back of his wagon?"

"That's right!" exclaimed Jenny. "The mob was going to hang him for killing a man, but Wyatt stood up to the crowd and told them no, they couldn't do that. He said that it was up to the court to decide if Johnny-Behind-the-Deuce was guilty or not."

"And what did you just see Wyatt Earp do?" asked the Swamper.

"He just murdered a man," said Luke. "He didn't give Frank Stilwell the chance to go to court and have a trial."

Chapter Twenty-Three
Wyatt Earp's Ride of Vengeance

Luke, Jenny, and the Swamper were back on Allen Street. It appeared to be late in the afternoon. Luke and Jenny were both still thinking about what the Swamper had pointed out: Wyatt Earp, who was supposed to be a lawman, had just killed a man in cold blood.

"I wonder what would have happened if Wyatt hadn't shot Frank Stilwell," said Jenny. "Do you suppose that if Wyatt had done the right thing and taken Frank Stilwell to jail instead, that we might have found out who really killed Morgan? And who shot Virgil, too?"

"We might very well have," answered the Swamper. "A lot of questions might have been answered. The guilty parties would have been hung, no doubt about that. But you see, no lawman ever has the right to make himself judge, jury, and executioner like Wyatt Earp just did."

"But Mr. Swamper," asked Luke, "since all of you are now spirit people, do you know who it was?"

The Swamper thought for a moment.

"Well, let's just say that not every spirit goes to the same place. And for whatever reason, some things we are just not meant to know."

He then explained that the killing of Frank Stilwell had outraged the citizens of Tombstone even more and that an arrest warrant had been issued for Wyatt and Warren Earp, Doc Holliday, and the others who had been in the rail yard that night.

In the meantime the wife of another Cowboy, Pete Spence, had come forward to testify at the coroner's inquest that she believed her husband, Frank Stilwell, and two other Cowboys—Hank Swilling and Indian Charlie—may have been the ones who killed Morgan Earp. Pete Spence was now in jail.

They walked up the Cosmopolitan Hotel and saw a group of men entering the building.

"That's the Earps and Doc Holliday," said Luke.

A man approached Wyatt with a telegram in his hand.

"The telegraph operator is a friend of Wyatt's," explained the Swamper. "He's warning him about the arrest warrant. The telegram is actually addressed to Johnny Behan, but he'll make sure to take plenty of time before getting it to him."

A moment later it was dark again. Then the Earps came out and started getting on their horses.

"Uh oh," said Luke, pointing up the boardwalk, "I see Johnny Behan coming."

Johnny Behan approached Wyatt just as he was getting on his horse.

"Wyatt, I want to see you."

Wyatt, sitting on his horse, looked down at Johnny Behan.

"You've seen me once too often." And with that he and the others rode away.

"Wyatt Earp is riding out of Tombstone for the very last time," said the Swamper. "And even though he'll live to be a very old man, he'll never once set foot in this town again."

"So what happened next?" asked Luke.

"What happens next will haunt Wyatt for the rest of his life," said the Swamper. "First, Johnny Behan will form a posse to go after the Earps. Riding with him will be such good upstanding citizens as the Clanton brothers and Johnny Ringo. But Wyatt has plans of his own. He's going to avenge his brothers and he'll leave a bloody trail behind. People will call this Wyatt Earp's Ride of Vengeance."

Suddenly, they were standing in the desert outside of town. They could see the Earp party off in the distance. They appeared to be chasing after someone. As they rode down a hill they vanished from sight. A few moments later they heard the sound of distant gunfire.

"The Earps have just gunned down a man named Florentino Cruz, who is also called Indian Charlie by some of his Cowboy friends. He's one of the men that Pete Spence's wife believed killed Morgan Earp."

"They didn't try to take him alive to stand trial?" asked Jenny.

"No," replied the Swamper. "By now, Wyatt has lost all faith in the legal system. So he's taken matters into his own hands."

"But that's still not right," said Jenny.

"I know," said the Swamper, "that's why Behan is trying to catch him. The funny thing is, if Wyatt were to get caught, he could end up being hung for murder himself."

"Even though he believes the men he's killed also killed his brother?" asked Luke.

"That's right, Luke," replied the Swamper. "Have you ever heard the saying that two wrongs never make a right?"

"Yes," said Luke.

"Well, this is exactly what it means. The men who murdered Morgan deserve to be punished for what they did. But Wyatt going after them and gunning them down makes him just as guilty as those who killed Morgan."

"And it won't bring Morgan back, either," added Jenny.

"No, I guess it wouldn't," agreed the Swamper. "But Wyatt's ride of vengeance is nearly over. And it will come to a very dramatic end."

Chapter Twenty-Four

Wyatt Earp's Final Showdown with the Cowboys

Luke, Jenny, and the Swamper were standing near a little watering hole called Iron Springs. They watched Wyatt and his friends come up to the creek to water their horses.

Suddenly shots were fired from the bushes on the other side of the creek. Jenny grabbed Luke by the shoulder and pulled him back. As they looked back up they saw several Cowboys opening fire on the Earps. A bullet hit one of the horses and it fell dead, pinning its rider underneath. Wyatt Earp leapt off his horse and looked back at his friends with a look of pure disbelief on his face. They were all riding away, leaving Wyatt to face the Cowboys alone.

"Look, Jenny!" exclaimed Luke as he pointed to the Cowboys. "It's our old friend, Curly Bill!"

"You're right, Luke," replied Jenny. "And look! Wyatt sees him, too."

Curly Bill began firing at Wyatt Earp.

"If I go down, I'm taking you with me!" shouted Wyatt as he raised his shotgun and fired at Curly Bill.

He fired the gun with both barrels. The rounds hit him square in the chest, and Curly Bill screamed as he fell.

The other Cowboys returned fire as Wyatt reached for his

rife in his saddle scabbard. But then his horse, frightened by the sound of the gunfire, started to rear, taking the rifle out of his reach. So Wyatt reached for his pistol and fired back into the brush.

He tried to get back on the horse but his gun belt had slipped from his waist and was wrapped around his thighs. That made it almost impossible to get back on.

The Cowboys kept firing as Wyatt, with one foot in the stirrup, tried to lift his gun belt with one hand while holding onto the frightened horse with the other.

"In a way, Wyatt is lucky this happened," said the Swamper. "All this moving around makes him a hard target to hit."

As the bullets kept whizzing past him Wyatt somehow managed to get his gun belt up and get back on his horse. He stopped long enough to help his friend, Texas Jack Vermillion, out from underneath his dead horse. Texas Jack leaped on the back of Wyatt's horse and the two raced away.

"Doc Holliday and the others couldn't believe that Wyatt and Texas Jack escaped in one piece," said the Swamper.

"It's just like that day near the O.K. Corral," observed Jenny. "Wyatt walked away without a scratch that day, too. My grandmother would probably say that Wyatt Earp has the luck of the Irish."

"So what happened then?" asked Luke.

"After that day at Iron Springs, Wyatt must have gotten his fill of killing. No other Cowboys died at his hand after that. Behan's posse kept after the Earps but they never caught up with them. Wyatt and the others eventually made their way to New Mexico, and then Wyatt went on to Colorado. He settled there for a time, but Wyatt never stayed in one place for too long."

"So Wyatt never went to trial?" asked Jenny.

'No," said the Swamper, "as far as I know, he never returned to Arizona. But his reputation would haunt him for the rest of his life."

He told them that Wyatt and his wife, Josephine, would spend the next 50 years seeking their fortune throughout the West. They would travel as far away as Alaska. And then, in his last days, Wyatt Earp lived in Los Angeles, working with some of the movie studios in Hollywood as a historical consultant.

"Wyatt Earp worked in Hollywood?" asked Jenny.

"Yep," replied the Swamper. "Wyatt died in 1929. At that time, silent movies were being made. In fact, one of the pall bearers at Wyatt's funeral was a famous silent movie star by the name of Tom Mix."

"What about Doc Holliday?" asked Luke.

"Doc died of Consumption in Colorado in 1886," said the Swamper. "As rough of a man as he was, he managed to die peacefully in his own bed."

"And Curly Bill?" asked Jenny.

"Funny you should mention him," said the Swamper. "Wyatt killed Curly Bill that day, but no one knows where he's buried. Remember when we went to Galeyville and you saw Jim Wallace shoot Curly Bill in the head?"

"Yes," said Luke.

"Well, because Curly Bill had survived that time, a lot of folks believed he'd survived this time, too. So there were stories of Curly Bill sightings for sometime afterward, but they were all just rumors. Curly Bill was never seen anywhere in or around Tombstone again."

"Except as a spirit person," added Luke. "Isn't he waiting for you to watch a ballgame at Big Nose Kate's?"

"Yep, he is," said the Swamper. "In fact, it's time for you to go back to Tombstone as well."

Instantly, they were walking down Allen Street once again. The Swamper told Luke and Jenny that another fire would soon come along, in May of 1882, and nearly burns the town down once again. And, just like before, the town would quickly rebuild and be back in business. But then the mines would later flood, and that event would mark the end of the boom town years. Tombstone would later become something of a ghost town, living on its memories.

"It's been called the Town Too Tough to Die," he said as they stopped in front of Campbell & Hatch's Saloon

"Well, it's nearly time for me to go. Your mother will be back soon, and I have to meet my friends at Big Nose Kate's. The baseball game's about to start."

"But I don't want you to leave," said Luke. "I want to stay here with you."

The Swamper smiled.

"You mean this really was more exciting than Disneyland?"

"Well..." replied Luke, "almost."

He gave the Swamper a big smile and started to laugh.

"It really was fun, Mr. Swamper, but I would rather live in my own time," said Jenny. "Still, I'm going to miss you. I hate saying goodbye to my friends, and now I think of you as my friend."

"And I think of both of you as my friends, too," said the Swamper. "But don't you worry. You two will come back to Tombstone again, and I'll always be here."

"Goodbye, Mr. Swamper," said Jenny. "And thank you so much for taking us back to your time. You were right. It really was an exciting adventure. Luke and I both learned a lot."

"Goodbye, Jenny," said the Swamper as he tipped his hat to her. "And goodbye, Luke. And don't worry about you father, Luke. He'll be coming home before you know it. Now you two have fun in Dallas."

The Swamper turned and started walking across the street toward the Grand Hotel. Then he stopped and looked back.

"Oh by the way, Luke, I'm sorry about your Game Boy."

"What?" asked Luke.

"Your battery," he said. "I had to drain it. You see, I needed to use the energy so you two could see me and the other spirit people, and to bring you to the past. But don't worry. All you have to do is recharge it, and it will work just fine."

"Thanks," said Luke as he sat back on the bench.

Then they saw the strange flash of bright light they had seen before. Afterward they were back in their own time. The horses were replaced by cars parked along the side roads.

"Look, Luke!" said Jenny, pointing across the street.

The Grand Hotel was gone. It was once again Big Nose Kate's Saloon. The Swamper waved goodbye, then turned to go inside Big Nose Kate's as he slowly faded away.

Chapter Twenty-Five
On to Dallas

Jenny joined Luke on the bench in front of Campbell & Hatch's. They both sat quietly for a few moments. Then she asked, "Luke, did all of that really just happen?"

"I don't know," he replied.

He stood up from the bench and looked up the boardwalk to see if he could spot their mother.

"Jenny, look at that," he said as he looked into the window of the shop that had once been Campbell & Hatch's Saloon.

"There's a pool table in there, right underneath the skylight. In the exact spot it was the night Morgan Earp was killed."

Jenny stood up and looked in the window.

"You're right, Luke," she said. "Maybe it really happened. Maybe we didn't just imagine it all."

They stood on the boardwalk a few minutes longer waiting for their mother. A voice behind them said, "Excuse me."

A handsome young man with a mustache wearing a fine looking suit from an earlier time was walking down the boardwalk with his dog. Luke and Jenny stepped out of his way and he smiled and tipped his hat to them as he passed by.

"Good afternoon, Jenny. Good afternoon, Luke."

"Good afternoon, Morgan," replied Jenny.

She looked back at her brother. Then their eyes opened wide as they both realized whom she had just spoken to. They looked back at the boardwalk, but Morgan Earp and his dog had vanished. Then they heard the distant sound of Morgan's laughter.

"I guess that means he's okay now, huh, Jenny?"

"I think so, Luke," she replied. "I think he just wanted to let us to know he's all right."

"Hey you two," said another voice behind them.

Luke and Jenny turned around.

"Mom!" they both said at the same time.

Ellen Bartlett's arms were full of shopping bags.

"Here Mom, let me help you," said Luke as he took a couple of the bags.

"Wow!" said Jenny. "It looks like you bought the whole store."

"Well I had to get a little something for everybody," she said as they walked to their car.

A man in cowboy clothes walked up to them.

"Howdy folks," he said. "There's a gunfight show this afternoon at the O.K. Corral."

"No thanks, we already saw it," said Luke.

Jenny gave her brother a strong look.

"You know, in the movies," he added.

At the car their mother handed them their presents while they put the rest of the bags in the trunk. She gave Jenny a t-shirt that said, "Tombstone" on the front and she gave Luke a baseball cap that also said, "Tombstone."

"Thanks Mom," said Jenny.

"Cool!" said Luke. "Thanks Mom."

They got into the car and buckled their seatbelts. Ellen started the car. Luke reached into his backpack and handed her the adapter for his Game Boy battery charger.

"Did you run the battery down already, Luke?" she asked.

"Yes," he replied.

She plugged the adaptor into the cigarette lighter.

"You and that Game Boy. You know, one of these days

Luke you're going to have to get out into the world and be around real people for a change."

Luke and Jenny looked at each other and started giggling as their mother backed out the car and pulled onto the street.

"Well, at least the two of you are in a better mood now. I guess you guys must have been hungry when we got here."

"That's right, Mom," said Jenny. She looked at her brother and smiled.

"You know how grumpy we get when we're hungry."

They made their way back onto the highway. Luke went back to playing with his Game Boy while Jenny wrote in her journal. A very private person, she much preferred to keep a handwritten journal rather than post her private thoughts on an Internet blog for all the world to see. As she reached into her backpack for her journal she felt something strange. She pulled it out. It was the handkerchief that Fred White had loaned her.

THE END

A GUIDE FOR PARENTS AND TEACHERS

Luke and Jenny's story may be fiction, but the things they experienced in Tombstone are all based on actual historical events. The following lessons serve as a guide and may be useful in helping your students learn more about the history of Tombstone, and the post Civil War American West.

1. **Ethics in the Old West**. The Cowboy Gang were known to be cattle rustlers and thieves. Yet many people in Tombstone put up with them because they were good customers for the saloons and shopkeepers. Ask your students if they think that being good customers for businesses was a good enough reason to excuse bad behavior. Discuss how their actions may have harmed the ranchers whose cattle was stolen. Ask them if they think the Cowboys should have been arrested and jailed as cattle thieves.

2. **Tuberculosis**. Doc Holliday suffered from Consumption, or Tuberculosis. Have your students research this disease. Instruct them find out exactly what Tuberculosis is. Have them discuss what part(s) of the body this disease attacks, what the symptoms are, and how this disease is spread. Ask them to research and discuss how doctors treated it back then, and how doctors treat it today. Discuss with your students why this disease is so rare today.

3. **The Right to a Fair Trial.** Wyatt Earp risked his own life to save Johnny-Behind-the-Deuce so he could have a fair trial. Ask your students what they think this right means. Discuss with them the reasons why our Founding Fathers determined the right to a fair trial so important, and what our lives might be like if

we did not have the right to a fair trial.

4. **Mining.** Tombstone was a mining town. Have your students research how the miners got the ore out of the ground. Ask them if mining was a dangerous occupation, and discuss what working conditions were like for miners in the Old West.

5. **Sports in the Old West**. Baseball was popular in the Tombstone. Have your students research the history of popular sports, such as baseball, football, basketball, or hockey.

6. **Gun Safety**. The shooting of Marshall Fred White was a terrible accident. Have a discussion with your students about what the Marshall could have done differently to have prevented this tragedy. Ask your students if they think Curly Bill should have been charged with murder. You may want to consider having a police officer or other safety expert come and talk to your class about gun safety.

7. **The Verdict**. Judge Wells Spicer ruled that the Earp Brothers and Doc Holliday were justified in their actions at the shoot out on Freemont Street. Discuss his ruling with your students and ask them if they agree with the judge. Ask them if they think that Ike Clanton's claim of the Earps and Doc Holliday being involved in the stagecoach robbery should have been investigated further.

References

Bell, Bob Boze. The Illustrated Life and Times of Wyatt Earp. Phoenix: Tri Star - Boze Publications. 2000.

Eppinga, Jane. Images of America: Tombstone. San Francisco: Arcadia Publishing. 2003.

Howell, Evelyn, Editor. Tombstone Chronicles: Tough Folks, Wild Times. Phoenix: Arizona Department of Transportation. 1998.

Tefertiller, Casey. Wyatt Earp: The Life Behind the Legend. New York: John Wiley & Sons, Inc. 1997.

Luke and Jenny's adventures continue in

Billy the Kid and the Lincoln Country War:
a Luke and Jenny Adventure.

Please visit our website at www.LukeandJennyBooks.com
for the latest news and information about Luke and Jenny.